FILIGREE AND FATE

TALES FROM THE FAE COURT - BOOK ONE

HELLUCY HOWE

STARDUST
EMPIRE
PUBLISHING

IN THE BEGINNING...

This novella originally appeared in the anthology *A Perfectly Paranormal Valentine*, released in February, 2021.

This amazing anthology is well worth a read - apart from Filigree and Fate, there are four other amazing stories to gorge on!

Check it out here:
https://books2read.com/u/bprDzg

*I give thanks to my fellow anthology authors
for sharing the wild trip:
Leisl, Marnie and Samantha,
who refused to give up on me.
Sam, I love you.*

CHAPTER ONE

ZHULIJA

*Z*hulija drifted down to the Eribifax mansion's welcome garden and closed her wings, noting with pleasure how many of the plants in this botanical nook mirrored her own. How naive of her to think the greenery would be different on this side of the river; plants were plants whether you were Seelie or Unseelie.

After twitching at her flutter-skirt, checking her bodice laces were still secured in a neat bow and assessing the safe attachment of her basket cover, she moved up the steps to the imposing front door, rapped the knocker and waited. The shape of the knocker called to the artist in her. Leaning closer, she traced the shape of the Dark Crimson Underwing Moth from which the Eribifax family had sprung, her fingers moving over the striations of the wings.

The door opened and she came face to midriff with a fae-male. A jolt shot up her fingertips as they moved across taut muscles. She snatched her hand back.

"By Old Lady Willow!" Zhulija straightened, cheeks blazing. "I do beg your pardon!"

"Are my muscles to your satisfaction, Lady?" A knowing smile revealed the fangs flanking his otherwise even front teeth. His lingering glance assessed her from head to toe, a widening grin causing dimples on his honey-coloured skin.

"I was studying your unusual knocker." Her flush deepened, but she refused to lower her gaze. "I have an appointment with Lady Eribifax, and I'm carrying a safe pass granted by the queens, which, I assure you, I had no intention of breaching." Her words died away as her focus locked on his deep grey eyes. She fell into a fathomless, comforting mist; it wreathed her, welcomed her, smoothed over her with soothing warmth and … Zhulija jerked and blinked.

"Come right in, pretty fae-lady. Your caresses didn't offend me in the slightest and our safe pass is intact. I'm very glad you found us." He bowed, arm sweeping an invitation.

The old fable of the spider inviting the fly into its parlour assailed Zhulija. "Oh, but I didn't mean to, um, stroke you, I just …" Stopping, she swallowed. "Again, sir, my pardon." Stepping past him, she heard the deep breath he drew. Like he was scenting her; how peculiar. Turning to face him, she lifted her chin. "Thank you, my appointment is with the Lady Catocala Eribifax."

Eyes soulful, his hands-to-chest motion was pure theatre. "I'm crushed, my Lady. I've been waiting for you forever."

"Oh, but I …" The ridiculous man was flirting with her. She clasped her basket tightly. "I really am here to see Lady Catocala."

"Of course, Lady Zhulija." Her doorman indicated the side table. "We can put your basket there as soon as I shove that ugly candelabrum aside." The reception hall calmed with earthy tones. Dark green marble tiled the floor, and there was a creamy green, marble side table against one wall, graced by a gold candelabra. Beige velvet drapes flanked the windows either side of the doorway.

She stiffened. "You … you knew who I was all the time!"

"But, of course. A visit from a Seelie lady via our joint queens' promise of safety is an interesting event." A tilt of the head accompanied his roguish smile. "Forgive me if I offend, but constant conversation about the upcoming wedding can pall on one." He winked. "And people with appointments have a name." He gripped the basket handle. "Allow me."

Zhulija's hand shot out, covering his on the basket. "Oh, no, it's perfectly fine."

His hand remained, and those downcast stormy eyes assessed her fingers on his skin before dark lashes lifted to impale her with heat. "Are you sure?"

He tugged.

She tugged back. "The basket contains samples to show Lady Catocala."

He cocked one eyebrow, staring. She shivered, but refused to be cowed, allowing her claw-tips out to infinitesimally pierce his flesh. At that, his hands slid away.

A smile broadening his firm lips, he turned. "This way to the old lady."

Shaking her head, Zhulija followed him down the hall. He didn't wear a uniform, so maybe he wasn't staff, but if he wasn't staff, then …

He leaned into an open doorway without bothering to knock. "My latest fan to see you, Mother."

"Really, Dario, your manners are execrable." A ruby-haired woman in a sparkling, violet robe sat at a desk. A pearl comb secured her up-do. "I doubt she is any fan of yours."

Face hot, but with a better understanding of his disrespect, Zhulija eased past the chuckling, tautly muscled Adonis filling the opening. "Thank you, Lord Eribifax." She closed the door in his grinning face.

"I apologise for any offense my son has given, Lady Zhulija."

"None taken, Lady Catocala." Zhulija smiled and accepted the seat the Unseelie matriarch indicated.

"Let's get started then, shall we?"

Removing the basket cover, she lifted out her samples, naming them as she placed them on the desk. "Filigree baskets to be filled with a plant, some macaroons, wrapped lollipops or chocolates, little pots of nectar, honey or jam, or whatever else you might like.

Blown-glass bowls to be filled with sand and flowers or floating candles. Smaller bowls can be made with flat surfaces to sit on tables or with hanging loops. Samples of handmade papers for invitations and place cards. Here is a filigree tube able to take one flower stem as a lady's brooch, or a buttonhole for males."

Lady Catocala reached for a lacy metal basket. "Such beautiful work, my dear." Her glance contained a sting. "I wonder that a renowned artist like yourself would stoop to crafting fripperies for weddings."

"The first wedding was a favour for a close friend." Zhulija smiled through tight lips. "Making lots of little bits and pieces is a way to relax whilst practicing my skills and thinking about my next major project. I find the muse works as it will."

"Yes, yes, I'm sure it does." Lady Catocala rotated the filigree basket. "Would you mind if my daughter Vinaya views your samples?"

"Not at all." Zhulija smiled. "I was surprised not to see her with you – it's her wedding, isn't it?"

Lady Catocala waved a hand as if to swat an insect. "Indeed." She lifted a handbell and melodic chimes echoed through the room. Moments later, the draperies behind the desk rustled apart to reveal a sliding door. A younger version of Lady Catocala danced through.

Vinaya Eribifax was smiling. Her wine-coloured hair tumbled over her left shoulder in waves, and a deep-teal robe offset the grey eyes and honeyed skin tones common to the Eribifax family.

"I'm so excited! Such a pleasure to meet you, Lady Zhulija. I love your work and to have you as my wedding consultant is simply wonderful. We weren't sure if you would agree, you know, since you're Seelie Lepidopter-fae and we're Unseelie, but here you are." The girl paused for breath, her wings flaring to reveal upper halves in shades of black, silver and cream and underwings of crimson edged with black. Vinaya clapped and reached for the samples. "Ooh, look at these delightful baskets – I can just see them on my tables." She did a tiny sidestep. "Or wait, no! The glass

4

bowls are delightful – can you create different colours in the glass, Lady Zhulija?"

"Yes." Zhulija made a note on her pad. "And the filigree baskets can be gold, silver, bronze, rose gold or copper. The papers can be whatever colour you choose."

"Do you write out the invitations and place cards yourself?" Lady Catocala steepled her fingers.

"No, but one of my sisters is a calligrapher. We often work together."

"Hmm." Lady Catocala watched her daughter, a genuine smile gracing her lips. "This is your choice, Vinaya?"

"Oh yes." Lady Vinaya did a pirouette. "I love Lady Zhulija's work. May I have the baskets in rose gold and hanging bowls in rose and lavender? Also, the filigree floral holders in rose gold? They'll look lovely on dove-grey formal coats."

As they worked out the particulars of the order, Zhulija retrieved the filigree flower holder, and tucked it behind her ear as she often did with a pen or paintbrush, clipping it to her hair to secure it. Other pieces she wrapped and tucked into her basket before re-tying the flight cover.

"It really is delightful having you decorate my wedding," Vinaya enthused. "Mycostat, my fiancé, will be so thrilled."

"That's wonderful." Zhulija smiled. "In the meantime, I'll begin crafting the items. Here's my card should you need to contact me for any reason."

"Thank you, I'll take that." Lady Catocala extended a hand. "Here's mine."

Zhulija was stooping to collect her basket when the door to the hall flew open, bounced off the wall and a fae-male wearing a uniform in Eribifax colours rushed in.

"Brax!" Lady Catocala glared. "What's going on? You dare interrupt?"

"My apologies, Lady Catocala. I didn't realise …" The fae-male saw Zhulija and his eyes narrowed. "She's here! The Seelie thief threatens the ladies."

As he leapt towards Zhulija, another two fae-males raced into the room. The sense of their malice swamped Zhulija in a wave of breath-stealing grey fog; a complete contrast to the warmth of her earlier welcome. She backed away from the hard fingers reaching for her, flailing at them with the basket. "I have a safe pass!"

The men paused.

"Brax?" One of the followers grabbed Brax by an arm.

"You can't believe a thief!" Brax shrugged off the restraint and charged again.

"What do you think you're doing, Brax?" Lady Catocala stood. "Unhand Lady Zhulija immediately!"

Brax ignored her as he reached out.

Zhulija's back met a wall; she couldn't avoid the reaching hands. She was jerked off her feet and forced to the floor. The hard surface smacked her forehead, shoulder and hip, before someone rolled her, face down and dug a knee into her back. The force was so intense, it caused her breath to shoot out in a winded croak. When the pain in her head chose that moment to surge, her mind fuzzed like dandelion puff balls caught in a tornado.

"Check the basket." The voice of Brax barely penetrated as she fought the dull bands around her chest, sabotaging her ability to breathe. Zhulija was helpless to resist her basket being wrenched over her wrist, but fresh pain freed the frozen muscles of her lungs and she gulped at air like a landed fish. An agonised cry left her at the new and fierce torment of her arm being thrust behind her back and forced upwards.

"Stop, I say, stop!" Lady Catocala's anger snapped like a whip.

"Dario, come quickly!" Vinaya cried.

Zhulija tasted blood, heard the sound of glass breaking – her samples? Helpless, breath rasping, she struggled, moaning as her arm was pushed towards the back of her skull and hot needles exploded through her shoulder. Footsteps thundered nearby.

"What in blue blazes is going on?" Dario roared over the din.

"We've an intruder, my Lord. A Seelie thief. She has your missing pen tucked behind her ear."

"You have my invited guest!" snarled Lady Catocala. "This is an outrage! Release Lady Zhulija at once!"

"Let her go!"

"But my Lord—"

"I said let her go!" Dario's hiss was a knife on whetstone.

The pressure on Zhulija disappeared. Her all but numb arm smacked to the tiled floor, the impact adding to the burning agony of her muscles. She couldn't stop the sob escaping.

"Lady Zhulija?"

Panting, lips trembling, she met the concerned gaze of Dario. "W-what's h-h-happening?"

"I'm so sorry they've hurt you, sweet lady." His eyes wandered over her face, before focusing somewhere near her left ear. Louder, he said, "A mistake has occurred, but I can see why they think you're a thief."

"Dario, are you mad?" Lady Catocala spat out. "There's no way that Lady Zhulija is a thief; she's been with either you or me the entire visit."

"Mother, a moment please." He reached out with gentle fingers to unclip and withdraw Zhulija's filigree flower holder from behind her ear. "I can see this isn't a pen – what is it?"

"A filigree flower holder!" Vinaya snatched it from him, then crouched to check on Zhulija. "Are you alright, Lady Zhulija? This is just awful."

Zhulija struggled to sit; the burning in her right arm and shoulder was excruciating. Dario reached to help, but she slapped his hands away, wincing as she clawed her way to her knees. Her eyes registered the remains of her samples, her smashed basket with the flight cover in tatters. A pulse of outrage brought tears to her eyes. Breath shuddering, wincing, she struggled to her feet.

"Lady Catocala, Lady Vinaya." She swayed, voice shaking. "Please accept my regrets, but I'm sure you'll understand my inability to fulfil your commission."

Lady Catocala flinched, her mouth taut. "I must apologise for this fiasco, Lady Zhulija."

Vinaya was crying. "Oh, Lady Zhulija, I had so wanted ... I'm so sorry."

"As am I. Good day." Every step Zhulija took hurt her aching body, but she pushed herself towards the front door, determined to remain polite.

"Wait!" Dario called.

"I don't think so, the safe pass was a lie and trusting it was a fool's choice."

Someone grabbed her arm and Zhulija's hurt morphed to rage. Hissing, she slapped her other hand upon the aggressor, her thoughts full of broken glass and smashed filigree.

"Aargh!"

"Dario, what happened?"

"She burned me."

"I'll get her, Lord Dario!"

"No! Leave her be, you've done enough damage."

Cradling her abused arm, Zhulija fled the chaos. Colliding with the door jamb, she blinked at the tears obscuring her vision as she staggered outside.

Diplomatic relations be damned – she had to get away.

Had to find safety.

She just needed a moment ...

CHAPTER TWO

DARIO

"Mab's tits!" Dario stared at the crisp filigree pattern seared into his honey-hued skin.

"My Lord, we can't let her get away with that." Brax jerked a thumb at his helpers. "We can make her pay."

"NO!" Dario lunged in front of them, fangs bared.

"But my Lord Dario ..."

"This house has fought for equality between the Seelie and Unseelie fae for generations – I'll not have your bigotry ruining it." Dario's voice deepened to a growl. "In fact, if any of you touch her, I'll rip your wings off."

The trio of footmen shrank from him, mouths gold-fishing.

"And I'll use those ripped off wings for wallpaper!" Lady Catocala swept forward to cradle Dario's hand. "You could get this magically healed or keep it and have a lovely scar. I'm sure it's painful." Her lips firmed. "Serves you right. I can't imagine you thought Lady Zhulija a thief." She snatched the filigree holder from Vinaya. "This looks nothing like the pen I gave you – which is on my desk, by the way. I borrowed it, and if you'd just bothered to ask around, this nastiness could've been avoided."

"I never considered Lady Zhulija a thief. All I did was curse

9

when I couldn't find my pen," Dario shook his head. "I didn't tell anyone to start a fae-hunt."

"Did you hear that, you stupid creatures?" Vinaya smacked Brax across the arm. "If I wasn't a lady, I'd be tempted to punch you all."

The other two footmen backed hastily away.

Lady Catocala's hands flashed to her hips. "Stop that at once, Vinaya."

Vinaya threw her hands in the air. "But everything is ruined!"

Dario pinched the bridge of his nose. "What's ruined, Vinaya?"

"My wedding on Valentine's Day." She glared. "Lady Zhulija had just agreed to make the reception decorations. I couldn't wait to tell Mycostat but now it's all spoiled. You and these oafs have ruined my wedding!"

Dario shook his head. "I had nothing to do with it." He assessed his stinging hand, liking the pattern, resistant to the idea of a healing. Maybe cold water would help.

"I'm afraid it's worse than that," Lady Catocala said.

Dario's gaze shot to her. "What do you mean?"

"Our idiotic footmen just assaulted Lady Zhulija Aphiski, who, I'm sure you know, is a daughter of Seelie Duke Papillion." She glared at the errant footmen. "Feuds have started with less provocation. How long do you think before it escalates to a full-blown Seelie versus Unseelie war?"

Dario closed his eyes. "Bat turds."

Vinaya's fangs flashed. "You'd better fix things for my wedding, Dario."

"For Mab's sake! I need to fix more than your wedding." Dario wheeled and pointed. "You three wait in my study. We'll talk about this fiasco later." He strode towards the front door.

"But Dario, you can't just leave!" Vinaya wailed. "Where are you going?"

"To find a way through this imbroglio; something I can't do if I stay here."

Dario slammed the front door, then paused to massage his

temple. What a troll-be-damned mess those blasted footmen had created. He'd have to fly to the Papillion Estate, seek audience with Duke Papillion and offer reparations. Would the Duke be amenable? He really needed to work on Lady Zhulija first. Would she be willing to see past both the injuries and the insult? He shook his head recalling her courage – distressed and injured, she'd still politely told them all where they could stuff themselves. He grinned. He'd liked that. She'd been injured, her clothing torn and rumpled, but she'd zapped him and swanned off like a princess.

Dario froze mid-step below the colonnaded veranda as he grappled with the extreme notion that he was attracted to her.

Peering over the hedge, Dario relaxed – she hadn't left. She'd fanned her sooty wings, with their splashes of green, cobalt, violet, cream and white, but she was yet standing in the welcome garden. He basked in her beauty, limned against the bright sky.

"Lady Zhulija." Was that frog croak his voice? He cleared his throat.

Snapping her wings shut, Zhulija faced him, black and violet hair fluttering about her shoulders. "What do you want now, Lord Dario? Haven't your people done enough to me?" The pearlescent caramel skin of her cheeks revealed a darkening blemish, tear tracks, and green-speckled violet eyes dull with pain.

Dario clenched his fists. Forget attraction – it was too mild a word for the feeling inside him. "Lady Zhulija, I need to apologise for the actions of my staff."

Zhulija crossed her arms. "You need to apologise, do you? Lady Catocala and Lady Vinaya were full of apologies. I'm a bit over them."

He closed his eyes for a moment. "I know, but it's all I have right now. I'm devastated you were assaulted and accused of theft over a misunderstanding."

She huffed a laugh. "A misunderstanding? That's what you're going with? I'm not sure I can accept that explanation, or your apology. Your people attacked me unprovoked. Is it because I'm Seelie fae? Do they still hold a grudge from the fae wars? They didn't know me, or what I was doing in your home, nor did they care. I even had the safe pass and it meant nothing."

He walked closer. "You have no idea how much I regret their actions. I can assure you they'll be dealt with."

She took a pace backwards. "Stop there."

He stopped. "I mean you no harm, Lady Zhulija. They thought the pen stolen, when in fact, my mother had borrowed it."

"I don't understand." Her hands spread. "What's so important about a pen, anyway? Apart from the gold?"

He grimaced. "It's an heirloom gifted to my grandfather by Nuada Silverhand of the Irish Tuatha de Dannan, centuries ago."

"The gift of a king." Zhulija nodded. "I can understand the concern, but not their attack. It wasn't necessary to hurt me and smash my belongings."

He winced. "Correct, and one of the reasons I'm apologising."

"One? Oh, I get it." She snorted. "Not only will your Queen Maerovana and my Queen Dianathke be angry, you're worried about offending the Duke of Papillion."

"My concern is for you." Even as he spoke, he was staggered to the depths of his Unseelie soul by how true that was. Dario wanted to cuddle Zhulija, smooth her hair, kiss the silvery path of her tears, nuzzle the bruises, lick her lips, kiss her until neither of them could remember their own names. It was both bewildering and overwhelming. He fought to understand; he had never cared about any of his past dalliance partners – what was different about Zhulija?

"Thank you for your concern."

"Your mouth looks swollen? Did they hit you there too?" He eased a step nearer.

"My mouth?" She frowned. "I've been biting my lips; it helps distract me from my shoulder and arm pain. I'm too sore to fly and I want to go home."

"Let me help you." Did he sound too eager? "I'll fly you home." A second infinitesimal step.

"I don't think so." She shook her head. "I might not survive if your help is anything like what happened earlier."

"Sorry can't possibly encompass the true depth of my feelings." Dario's desperation grew. "I'm not the one who hurt you. Please let me fly you home. While we're flying, I'll grovel some more."

A weak gasp of laughter from Zhulija. "Grovel? You? I don't think you're the grovelling type."

Dario sidled closer. "Will you please accept my apology, Lady Zhulija? Allow me to fly you home?"

She ignored his request, but her gaze pierced him. "Tell me why you're apologising?"

"For your treatment by my footmen, your injuries, your pain." He eased a little closer.

"That's all?"

He flung his arms wide. "Mab's tits, woman! What more do you want?"

She reached up and tapped the tip of his nose. "Better language for a start. And what about my samples? My basket?"

Closing his arms tightly around Zhulija, Dario fought a triumphant grin as he spread his wings and leapt skywards. "I apologise for your samples and your basket being broken. I'll even apologise for my language."

She gaped. "Are you ill?"

Laughing, he headed for the river. The Rubiconia was the Seelie/Unseelie border, its water neutral territory. "No, just trying to distract you, and it worked. I'm flying you home, aren't I?"

Zhulija looked around. Their kind were as comfortable in the sky as on the ground. She sagged. "You win. Thank you for flying me home." Her words were silk soft, gentle as a whisk of fur.

The urge to protect her firmed inside him. "Do you accept my apologies, Lady Zhulija?"

"Are you going to keep plaguing me until I do?"

"Definitely." He made his words a caress of velvet. Silvery, deep and rich.

Zhulija shivered, avoiding his eyes. Tightening his arms, he admired the black and purple colours of her hair, the sweep of lashes on her cheek and the shape of her ruby lips as he flew over the Rubiconia River border. He registered the neutral Isle of Garadenya to their right, bifurcating the river for a furlong, with its castle-fortress that had been empty for several generations. It was not much further to the Papillion Duchy with its sweeping willows around a wide, shallow lagoon.

"Should I land outside the gates?"

She was frowning. "Is it okay for you to be in Seelie territory?"

"Fortunately, our queens wrote the safe pass as a two-way permit."

Her glance was unreadable. "Could you set me down outside the green gazebo this side of the forest?"

"Across the boundary but not right to the front door? Won't that sound an alarm?"

"Not while I am with you. I wish to go to the gazebo – it's my studio."

"Ah, your studio." Dario nodded. "Of course. I know you'll want to start on my sister's wedding decorations straight away, but don't you think you should rest for today?"

"What?" Zhulija gaped at him. "You know I'm no longer doing Vinaya's wedding."

"You refused the commission because of the attack on you. I've apologised for that. Profusely. I've grovelled. I've flown you home safely. I plan reparations. Couldn't you change your mind about Vinaya's wedding?" He dropped down to a smooth landing next to the gazebo steps.

She stared at him, before shaking her head. "No, the whole idea was a mistake."

"Please?"

She frowned, still shaking her head.

"Pretty please?"

"I. Said. No." Her lips were a straight line.

"Why not? Didn't I apologise prettily enough?" He fluttered his eyelashes. "Please, beautiful maiden, I—"

"Alright!" She rolled her eyes. "I accept your apologies, but I won't change my mind about Vinaya's wedding."

"I didn't just give you half of an apology." He cocked his head. "Are you afraid? I pledge your full safety. I will even be your bodyguard to ensure it."

A wrinkle of her nose. "Nothing you say will alter my decision."

"Damn." He ran a hand through his tricoloured hair. "What about something I do then? Something to make up for the damage to you and your property?"

Zhulija stamped her foot. "What part of 'No' don't you understand? Is it the N? Or is it the O? You couldn't say or do a single thing to make me change my mind."

He grinned as her opposition triggered an unexpected blossoming inside his soul, which caused his previous attraction to be trumped by primal recognition. He'd more than met his match, he'd met his true mate. "Challenge accepted, sweet Zhulija."

"What? What challenge?"

His wings spread. "Besides, you owe me for burning my hand."

A blaze sparked in her eyes. "*I owe you?*"

"I'm so glad you see things my way." He winked, his psyche ablaze with joy. "I'll be back, my Lady Zhulija. Prepare to make wedding decorations. I'll tell Vinaya you're on it." Flexing his wings, he left the ground.

"You're not listening to me!"

Dario grinned as he looked down. "Your voice is a delight, I'll be happy to listen to it forever." Dipping his wings, he wheeled towards the river.

"You arrogant Unseelie oaf!" Zhulija's scream drifted to him. "What's wrong with you? We'll see about a challenge! I'll sort you out, you just wait!"

He was so looking forward to that.

CHAPTER THREE

ZHULIJA

"Good evening." Stepping into the dining room, Zhulija tilted her head to disguise the bruising on her left cheek, certain it blazed like a star. Her siblings were already seated at the table. She braced for interrogation.

"Punctual as always," Lyssica said, winking. Janeska grinned over her glass of sherry-nectar, Tindresse waggled her fingers and Armelle blew a kiss.

"At least we can eat now," groused her eldest brother, DeMaksim.

"Just because you're a bottomless pit." Treymeron moved nimbly to avoid his brother's fist.

"DeMaksim Aphiski!" Their mother, Duchess Azura, turned from the window where she was standing with Duke Yanvian to glare at her eldest son. "Your siblings are to be protected, not preyed upon."

"Yeah, don't 'prey upon' me, DeMaksim," jibed Treymeron, grinning. "Don't you know I'm vulnerable?" He chortled as DeMaksim flipped him off behind their mother's back.

"Vulnerable!" Janeska and Tindresse both hooted with laughter, then hi-fived each other.

"You're about as vulnerable as a porcupine," Armelle shook her head.

"And just as cuddly, I hear." Lyssica wrinkled her nose.

"What?"

"Really?"

"Who'd you hear that from?"

Lyssica waved a hand airily. "I never divulge my sources, darlings, but I hear Chinoserie Douglas was unhappy."

"Chinoserie Douglas?"

"You were trying to cuddle Chinoserie Douglas?"

"No!" Treymeron grimaced and made a gagging noise. "Don't be ridiculous."

"I'll tell her you said she's ridiculous," Lyssica threatened.

Treymeron pointed at her. "You do and I'll tell Grenade Helioze you reckon he has a wart on the end of his nose."

"You lying piece of ..."

"That's enough!" The whiplash of Duchess Azura's voice silenced them.

Zhulija watched her mother's threatening gaze move across the angelic, innocent visages of her siblings. Who were they trying to convince?

Zhulija wasn't surprised when her father crossed the room to put an arm around her shoulders, but the pressure caused her to wince.

"Are you alright, Zhu?" His concern warmed her.

"Of course." She didn't turn her head.

He scanned what he could see of her face, then nodded. "Let's join our wild bunch and eat dinner, hmmm?"

Duchess Azura glided over. "There you are, Zhu."

"Hi, Mama." Zhulija twisted to keep her mother on her right. After a cheek kiss, the Duchess grasped the hand held out by her consort and they moved to the table.

After they were seated, Zhulija served herself food from the platters being passed and pretended to eat, the chatter of her family flowing around her like a comforting blanket. She listened to DeMaksim reporting on estate management lessons and Armelle talking about her music students, but the conversation faded into the background as she played with her food. Chewing hurt her bruised face, plus her wrenched right arm and shoulder made controlling cutlery awkward.

Duke Yanvian tapped a fork against his water glass. "Quieten down, please. Your mother and I wish to hear how Zhulija's meeting turned out."

"Yes, were the Eribifax Matriarch and her daughter impressed with your samples?" Duchess Azura turned an expectant smile on her youngest child.

"Oooh." Janeska winked. "Did you see that dreamy Lord Dario Eribifax, by any chance?"

"Dreamy?" Treymeron chuckled. "Have you missed the fact that he's also called the Unseelie Beast? He's reputed to be vicious to enemies."

Duchess Azura frowned. "Not now, Trey."

Zhulija attempted a smile. "Yes, they were impressed, and yes, I saw Lord Dario. It was strange crossing the Rubicon to Unseelie territory, but nothing happened."

"Really." Duke Yanvian sipped his wine. "So, where'd you get that bruise?"

She forced her eyes wide. "Bruise? I have a bruise?"

He snorted. "Unless you're going to suggest that's paint on your face?"

"Oh, this little mark?" Without thinking, Zhulija raised her left hand, forgetting how sore she was. She flinched.

"Zhulija? What happened?" Trust Maman to notice.

She sighed. "I fell." Mostly true. "Tripped on a rug I hadn't noticed. Hit my cheek and landed with my right arm twisted behind my back." Zhulija played with her fork. "Knocked the wind out of myself, wrenched my arm and my shoulder." Flipping her good hand palm up, she glanced from one family member to another.

"You're a terrible liar, Zhu." DeMaksim shook his head. Next to him, Tindresse's eyes were rolling and, in her peripheral vision, Armelle and Lyssica were nudging each other.

"Do you know you babble when you're inventing a story, Zhulija?" Duke Yanvian tilted his head. "It gives you away every time, no matter how plausible your fabrication."

Defeated, Zhulija closed her eyes.

"What really happened?"

"I …" A tear trickled.

Her mother poured tea into a fluted cup, spooned a little nectar into it and passed it across the table to her. "Why don't you explain what occurred at the Eribifax Estate, Zhu honey?"

Tea was her mother's answer to all the world's ills. Zhulija dashed the lone tear from her cheek, claimed the cup and sat, staring into the golden liquid.

"Zhu?"

"It started off well." She crumpled a napkin.

"So you've said." Duke Yanvian stirred his own tea.

"That's truth." Zhulija touched the cup to her lips but the tea was hot. She put it down. "My muse was fascinated by the door knocker design, I bent to study it. I was running fingers over it when the door opened and then I was stroking a man's stomach."

Her siblings howled with laughter.

"That poor butler." Janeska laughed, clapping her hands.

Zhulija shook her head. "It was Lord Dario, not the butler."

"Dario Eribifax answered his own front door?" Treymeron goggled at her. "I'd never do that."

"You don't do much of anything." Tindresse made a face at him. Trey answered with a rude finger gesture.

"Tindresse! Treymeron!" Duke Yanvian glared at both of them.

"Did you trace out his six pack while your hand was glued to his tummy, Zhu?" Armelle giggled into her hand.

"I explained and apologised." Zhulija's face was burning.

"Look at you blush." Lyssica's green fingernail pointed. "He must be even dreamier up close and personal."

"Lyssica, that's not ladylike." Duchess Azura tapped Lyssica's hand with a teaspoon. "Please behave."

"Zhulija?"

Her father was giving her 'the look'; Zhulija knew there was no escape. "Lady Catocala and Lady Vinaya were thrilled with my samples. They offered a contract."

"You do lovely work, Zhu." Janeska smiled. "They'd have to be mad, or stupid, if they didn't want to hire you."

"Very true," agreed Duke Yanvian. "Go on."

Unhappily, Zhulija related the events.

"What!" Her father's roar was so loud the windows rattled. "They attacked you?"

She cringed, unable to distinguish her mother's words when noise from her siblings drowned everything else out. "Please stop." She covered her ears. "Let me finish."

Her father thumped the table until all sound ceased. "Keep it down."

"Continue, Zhu." Her mother's voice was butter soft. She patted her husband's forearm.

"Lady Catocala and Vinaya called for Lord Dario."

"What did he do?" Duke Yanvian's face was thunderstorm dark.

"He made them stop." Zhulija rubbed her nose. "Then helped me roll over and saw the filigree flower holder in my hair."

"Oh, Zhu," DeMaksim murmured. "You always tuck that sample behind your ear."

She nodded. "Lord Dario knew straight away it wasn't his pen and I hadn't done anything wrong. He showed it to his footmen, but the damage had been done."

"Your injuries?"

"And all my samples smashed." Zhulija sniffled. "I wish my power was more than artistic so that I could've defended myself against those judgmental trolls."

DeMaksim's hiss was a sizzle of cold water on hot stone. "Defensive power isn't all it's cracked up to be, Zhu, and your art is a fae treasure."

"The whole business is outrageous." Tindresse's teaspoon clattered in the saucer. "They hurt you; something needs to be done."

Treymeron grinned, rubbing his hands together. "We're going to war against the Eribifax!"

"Don't be foolish, Treymeron!" Duke Yanvian glared. "We're not going to war. We'll request an apology and reparation."

"Lord Dario apologised several times and has offered reparation." Zhulija's voice cracked. "Please, no fighting. I couldn't bear it."

"There'll be no war." Duke Yanvian frowned at his youngest son.

Her mother smoothed the damask cloth. "Did you accept his reparation offer?"

"Not exactly." Zhulija's head began to throb as she stumbled through her edited explanation.

"So Lord Dario apologised profusely, assisted you home, then took your negative response as a challenge to be overcome?" Duke Yanvian's brow furrowed. "An interesting man. One I will be speaking to, particularly since the two-way safe passage agreement was breached on its first usage."

"Oh, but Father ..."

Zhulija's father speared her with 'the look'. She swallowed.

"This is a serious matter, Zhulija." Duke Yanvian's eyes never wavered from her own. "You were assaulted despite our safe pass, jointly approved by Queen Maerovana and Queen Dianathke. The ramifications threaten all Lepidopter-fae; these actions need careful finessing to avoid a pointless war."

She quivered. "I know."

"Ssh, Sis. It'll be okay." DeMaksim's gentle hand on her shoulder was comforting, but still painful.

"I-I ..." Zhulija's gulping sobs escaped despite her best efforts. Duchess Azura was there in an instant, gathering her into a warm cuddle. Her sisters clustered about, stroking her hair.

Duke Yanvian cleared his throat. "And the contract for the wedding supplies?"

Red-eyed and weeping, she met his expectant look. "I-I repudiated it."

"That's my sister!" Treymeron crowed, pumping his fist.

"B-but I w-wanted it!"

Her mother kissed her temple. "We know you're keen to consult for an Unseelie family; a resumé highlight for certain."

"Lord Dario kept asking me to reconsider."

"And will you?" Her father pursed his lips.

"Lady Vinaya chose nice pieces for her reception. I'd like to."

"How about Lord Dario? Is he a nice piece?" Grinning, Janeska patted Zhulija's cheek.

Zhulija stiffened, colour flowing from neck to cheeks.

"Oooh, she's blushing!"

"What's he like, Zhu?"

"Is he strokable?"

She recalled the electrical jolt of that first touch and something roared a protest inside her. Zhulija flicked her gaze from sister to sister. "Keep your claws off him."

CHAPTER FOUR

DARIO

innowing fingers through his hair, Dario released a pent-up snarl. "Before we start, let me remind you all that, as Queen Maerovana's appointed representative in this demesne, I have the power to use whatever means I deem necessary to access the truth of any crime. Those powers include truth reading, physical persuasion and incarceration." His molten gaze pinpointed each fae-man in turn. "Now, explain to me why molesting a Seelie lady of impeccable birth and reputation, who held an authorised safe pass into our lands, was considered an intelligent move."

"You said your pen was missing." Brax wrung his hands. One of his helpmates flinched, the other closed his eyes.

"Did I say it was stolen? Did I tell you to attack an innocent guest?"

"You've ruined my wedding!" Vinaya wailed from her window seat next to their mother.

"Be quiet, Vinaya!" Lady Catocala sighed.

"Brax?"

"I was trying to help, my Lord."

"Creating a diplomatic incident is helping?"

Brax held his hands out. "I didn't know who she was!"

"How is that relevant? You're saying if you'd known her identity, events would have been different? In what way?"

Brax stared at him, opened his mouth, closed it, then shrugged.

"Jern? What do you have to say for yourself?" Dario focused on the next man.

"My Lord, I can only apologise." Jern was pale and quivering. "When Brax said a nasty Seelie woman had gotten in, stolen your gold pen and was holding the ladies hostage in the anteroom, I leapt to assist him. I wasn't aware he'd lied."

"What?" Dario's brows shot skywards. "That's what he told you?"

"Y-yes, my Lord." Though pale, Jern met Dario's blazing eyes.

Thrusting out a tendril of mental energy, Dario assessed the man's mind. Truth. Tapping his claw-tips on the desk, he looked for the third footman. "Corab, come out from behind Brax."

Adam's apple bobbing, Corab sidled into view. He stood tall, the bloom of youth still in his cheeks. "Sir, me Lord, I thought as I was helping. Mr Brax told me the same as Jern here and I-I …" His lip quivered, but when Dario mentally truth checked, his version of events was solid.

Dario's eyes narrowed. "Anything to add Brax? Care to explain why you bamboozled Jern and Corab with a pack of lies?"

"I was only telling them what I'd heard."

"Heard from whom?"

Brax's eyes shifted away. "I can't rightly remember, my Lord."

"How convenient." Fuming, Dario conducted a truth search through Brax's public thoughts and found the fae-man's mind to be a seething morass of jealousy and hatred. Digging a little deeper, he discovered a strong belief of Seelie inferiority and bitter disagreement that the civil war of the previous generation had ended in a truce. He didn't sort through it all, but the reasons for the lies were obvious.

"My Lord, I apologise and I promise to do better."

"Better?" Dario slammed his fist on the desktop. "You're very lucky you didn't do any worse, Brax. You're a traitorous, conniving liar who committed unprovoked assault on a royally approved guest." His teeth clenched. "I refuse to employ such a person."

"She's just a woman, my Lord. A Seelie woman at that." An ingratiating smile. "A written apology will surely suffice."

Grinding his teeth, Dario shot around the desk and grabbed his prey by the throat. "She's not just a woman, you bigoted, overzealous idiot! She's my woman and you hurt her." Dario shook him. "Never mind you're making a mockery of the queen's orders, in an action capable of restarting the war!"

Brax's eyes bulged as Dario's clawed hand dug into his throat. He gurgled something.

Hair a fiery nimbus, Dario bared lengthening fangs.

"Dario!" Lady Catocala poked him in the back with her cane. "Back down. You can't shred the lackwit until Queen Maerovana is consulted about the violation of her personally signed safe pass."

Roaring, Dario flung Brax away. The fae-male sailed backwards to smash into the wall. The smell of urine wafted. Dario's vicious glare swivelled to encompass Jern and Corab. Jern was gasping and Corab shaking, but neither of them cowered.

"Remember they were manipulated, Dario."

Swallowing, Dario closed his eyes, fought the out-of-control rage.

Lady Catocala tapped her cane. "Jern and Corab, you've been misled by a traitorous liar, so we'll give you a second chance. Return to your duties. Please request Suitilay to attend us."

"Yes, my Lady." Jern turned from Lady Catocala back to Dario. "Nothing like this will ever happen again, my Lord."

Dario, in the middle of a breathing exercise, only grunted.

Corab never took his eyes from Dario. "Thank you, me Lord. Me life is yours, Sir me Lord."

"How right you are." Dario opened his eyes. "Don't disappoint us again." But it was not Corab's life he hungered for. Claws scraping the desk, Dario focused his eagle-sharp attention on Brax. The fae-man gulped, but stood stone still. Wise prey.

Suitilay appeared in the doorway. "Your will, Lord Dario?"

"This creature dishonoured the safe pass I secured from our queen by attacking an honourable Seelie lady without provocation. He also concocted a tale of falsehoods to convince two of our junior footmen to join him. Prepare him for transport."

"Ah, of course, my Lord, you wish the queen to interview him." Suitilay nodded. "Very appropriate."

"Go to Queen Maerovana?" Brax shivered.

"Aye." Dario's tongue swept his fangs. "I'm sure she'll be interested to hear how you made her into a liar. Don't you think, Brax?"

"No! I thought you'd—"

"You didn't think at all!" Dario thumped his fist on the desk. "You've failed to justify your actions to me, now you can explain yourself to Queen Maerovana. Tell her how you defiled her given word and threatened centuries of accord between the Seelie and Unseelie Lepidopter-fae."

"She has no mercy!" Brax backed away but stilled at Dario's animalistic growl.

"You think I have? After you besmirched the reputation of Family Eribifax and hurt my woman? I've not been named the Unseelie Beast for nothing. If there's anything left of you after our queen's through with you, I'll be happy to show you why." Dario's hair glowed like a furnace. "Take this scum-larva away please, Suitilay."

"As you wish, my Lord Dario." Suitilay fisted his chest.

"But she'll kill me!" Brax gripped fistfuls of his hair.

"And if war results from your behaviour, I'll string my bow with twine made from your guts!" The windows rattled with Dario's roar.

"Allow me to remove him from your presence, my Lord Dario." Suitilay dug twig-thin fingers into Brax's collar and yanked the footman off-balance. Brax's heels drummed on the tile as he was dragged from the room.

"Oh, and Brax?" Dario bellowed. "Just in case it wasn't clear – you're excommunicated from the Eribifax Family. We'll not be associated with treason." He listened as the wails faded down the corridor. When a slamming door cut off the irritating noise, he was flooded with vicious satisfaction. He ignored the shuffle of feet from behind him – there were plans to make, people to see …

"Dario?" Lady Catocala used her cane as a cattle prod.

"Ouch!" He rubbed his hip. Turning his head, he gave his mother the evil eye.

"Turn that burning glare off." She prodded him with her cane again.

He blinked, sighing as he reined his powers in. "Yes, Mother?"

"You handled that well."

He shook his head. "I was so close to sinking in claws and fangs, I could taste him …"

"But you didn't. Under the circumstances, no one would have blamed you."

"Circumstances?"

"You called Lady Zhulija your woman, more than once. Is that truth? Lady Zhulija is your mate?"

His eyes widened. "Blue blazes!" He sagged against the nearest object as dots connected in his mind. "Of course she is. That's why I was so drawn to her, why her welfare was so important to me, and why her scent was so thrilling. Mab's tits! But how does an Unseelie/Seelie connection come to be? What is Fate playing at?"

"What delightful irony!" His mother's brilliant smile was unexpected but genuine.

His eyebrows shot up. "You don't mind her being Seelie?"

"I'm not the treasonous bigot that useless wight is." She snorted. "Moreover, your father didn't fight and lose his mind, in a war aimed at uniting the two halves of the fae into a whole, because he believed in prejudice. It's more relevant if I ask; do you mind?"

He pictured Zhulija, and a smile creased his face. "No, she's a delight. Why would I care?"

"I'm glad you don't." Lady Catocala huffed. "There are still too many pockets of rebels and troublemakers for my liking."

Dario's mouth flat-lined. "Which is why the border watch is vigilant and why I ordered them to show no mercy."

"In any case, congratulations!" Lady Catocala shifted forward. "I'm more than thrilled you've found your mate. True mates are rare and precious, no matter the source. Does she know?"

"Not yet as far as I'm aware."

Lady Catocala wagged a finger. "Well, remember, under fae-law you can't take away her right of choice by telling her."

"I know, but it's not a law I ever expected to be subject to."

Vinaya did a little pirouette. "Dario, it's wonderful! Your children will be half Seelie and half Unseelie, just like the original Valentine!"

His eyes widened. "The original Valentine? What in the name of Queen Mab are you talking about?"

"Valentine was the child of a Seelie/Unseelie relationship and was constantly persecuted. Seelie fae hated his Unseelie blood while Unseelie fae hated his Seelie blood. He should have become a Lost-soul fae but instead campaigned his whole life for acceptance and love for everyone, regardless of race or creed. He was the first Neutral Fae. He and his loving consort died within hours of one another; it's said they couldn't face the world without the other half of their soul. In their memory, the legendary Queen Morgana created Valentine's Day. It's such a romantic story! That's why Mycostat and I chose Valentine's Day for our wedding gala."

Dario groaned. Romance. He would have to do romance. He wasn't sure he knew what that was.

Snapping his wings closed, Dario strode boldly to the guard house at the gates of the Papillion Estate. He flexed one hand as the breeze ruffled his shoulder-length hair clear of his face before tickling the pointed ears common to all fae. Pointing artfully in multiple directions, the attractive, youthful, just-out-of-bed hairstyle caused people to underestimate him. Time spent considering what to wear had resulted in charcoal leather form-fitting trousers, tucked into his favourite, calf-high boots. He flicked a flower petal from the sleeveless silver tabard that accentuated his muscular frame from shoulder to thigh and displayed the emblem of Clan Eribifax across his chest. The ensemble reflected his wing colouration and was completed by a low-waisted charcoal belt, supporting two well-used short swords on either hip. Anyone viewing those would be reminded that he was also known as the Unseelie Beast; not one to be trifled with. The darker charcoal cloak flowing from his shoulders rippled like low-lying thunder clouds.

Two guards stepped forth to cross swords in front of him. Another pair waited a couple of paces further back. He did the expected and stopped.

"Lord Dario Eribifax. I don't have an appointment with Duke Papillion, but I believe he will be keen to meet with me."

"Your Lordship." The blonde guard bowed. "We'll have to check with His Grace. Apologies for the delay."

"I understand." He did. Perfectly. His own guards would react in similar fashion if a Seelie Lord, or any stranger, showed up at his gates; otherwise, they'd be failing their responsibilities. He watched the four guards whispering amongst themselves before one spread his wings and sped towards the manor.

He neither spoke, moved nor relaxed as he waited. Two of the guards tried to watch him but couldn't hold his stare. They kept swallowing, shuffling their feet and glancing at their leader – the blonde who had spoken to him. That one maintained a watch that went past where Dario stood, feet firm, eyes intent.

Although the blonde appeared to be ignoring him, Dario sensed that his attention was as equally on the Unseelie lord waiting at the gate as it was on the path that vanished into the forest nearby. Likely suspicious of an attack, finding it difficult to believe that an Unseelie fae-lord was brave enough to visit alone. If the tables were turned, Dario would be the same.

Facing the estate, Dario was first to see the messenger returning.

"Open the gate! His Grace confirms his appointment with Lord Eribifax."

Dario felt a mirthless smile tugging at his lips. Oh yes, Duke Papillion certainly wanted to see him.

The Duke was waiting in his office, along with a younger fae-male. Dario looked for signs of Zhulija's heritage and identified it in hair and eyes. Unlike Zhulija, the green in Duke Papillion's eyes was dominated by violet striations, whilst his black hair was sprinkled with both blue and violet splotches. The younger male, with his identical features and colouring, looked to be a son. Dario discounted the pair being together as a show of force; he was unexpected, no matter what they told staff.

"Thank you for agreeing to see me, Your Grace." He swept a deep bow. "Lord Dario Eribifax at your service."

Duke Yanvian nodded. "Well met, Heir-Lord Eribifax." He indicated the younger male next to him. "My eldest, Heir-Lord De Maksim Aphiski." Dario met icy eyes set in a fierce frown. They exchanged polite bows despite the anger vibrating from Heir-Lord DeMaksim.

"I thank you for seeking me out, Heir-Lord Eribifax, since we have serious things to discuss. I assure you, if you hadn't arrived here within a four day, I'd have come looking for you." A wintry smile. "Which wouldn't have been pleasant."

Dario bowed again. "I understand such feelings, Your Grace. I tender my deepest apologies for the terrible wrong done to Lady Zhulija and beg your forgiveness."

"You understand?" Duke Yanvian's lips twisted. "Have daughters, do you, Heir-Lord Eribifax?"

Dario winced. "Um, no, Your Grace, but I have a sister." He sighed. "I'd be just as horrified and angry were similar treatment meted out to her. Again, I apologise. I seek to make reparation for the ill behaviour of my household. I'm empowered to speak on behalf of my mother, the Matriarch Eribifax."

"And how is the delightful Lady Catocala faring?"

"Well, Your Grace."

"And the miscreants who visited this gross misconduct upon my youngest daughter?"

"Dealt with, Your Grace." Dario detailed the interview he'd conducted and the results. His barely tamped fury surged beneath its shield and the crimson in his hair fired to an iridescent blaze.

De Maksim's eyes went wide.

"You sent the ringleader to Queen Maerovana?" Duke Papillion blinked. "I'd not expected that, Heir-Lord Eribifax."

Dario's low snarl vibrated in his throat and prowled the room. "He was also disowned by the Eribifax Family. My father fought beside you in the war to unite the fae and I'm equally as passionate as he was. I went to great trouble to secure Lady Zhulija's safe pass from the queens, affording her as much protection as possible from those pockets of resistance wishing to fracture our peoples and reinstate the old cultural barriers. The dishonour was treasonous, and Family Eribifax is loyal to its queen."

"Your father was a fearsome warrior and a delightful friend. I mourn his passing." Duke Papillion raised an eyebrow. "As for you, I'm impressed that the son of my old friend is dedicated to upholding the values his father held dear. Your prowess in confronting the rebel factions is widely renowned."

"You do me too much honour and I thank you for those cherished words about my father." Dario bowed." Shall we now talk about the point of my visit?"

Duke Papillion nodded. "Let's sit first, shall we?"

Dario accepted DeMaksim's offer of a chair. "We're agreed that Lady Zhulija was wronged, that my family owes her an apology plus reparations and that I'm correct in coming to see you." Dario ran a hand through his hair. "I've punished the offenders, apolo-

gised several times to both Lady Zhulija and yourself and
commenced reparations …"

"Commenced?" The Duke's eyes fastened on the filigree scar
decorating Dario's hand.

"I offered help when she was in pain." His memory of her
suffering still filled him with anger. "I flew her back here."

"So you did," Duke Yanvian agreed. "Then tried to coerce her
into making artwork for your sister's wedding as if nothing had
happened."

Dario frowned. "Coerce?" He shook his head. "Now there, we
disagree, Your Grace. I requested she consider changing her mind
about repudiating the contract – yes. I'm still trying to please my
sister, who insists her wedding has been ruined, after all. But I only
asked after I'd apologised that number of times and assisted Lady
Zhulija home. I'd already promised reparation and still plan to
keep that promise, no matter what she decides."

"Hmmm. If I accept all that, Heir-Lord Eribifax, may I ask what
you have in mind for reparations?"

"Of course, and I will answer as soon as I have my plans fully
prepared. At the moment, I foresee a number of items spread out
over a period of time. Perhaps flowers to start with, as is fae tradition. My sister's wedding is planned for Valentine's Day, and whilst
reparations for Lady Zhulija are high on my priority list, so is a
family wedding in two seven-days' time. As a family fae-person, I
trust Your Grace understands."

"Is Lady Vinaya difficult then?"

Dario's grimace was rueful. "More like spoiled, Your Grace."

For the first time, the second Papillion Family male proved
himself to be more than a statue. He snorted. "We've a few spoiled
family members too. I commiserate, Heir-Lord Eribifax, and thank
you for your care of my youngest sister."

"I'd like to believe any decent fae-male would be pleased to help
a lady in distress, and yet, someone my family considered a decent
fae-male behaved like a cave-troll to her." His lips wrinkled in a
fang-revealing growl. "I wanted to rip him to pieces."

DeMaksim cocked his head. "Yet you sent him to Queen Maerovana?"

Dario snorted. "My mother intervened."

A laugh escaped DeMaksim. "Ah yes, mothers." He nodded in complete accord.

Even Duke Yanvian's lips were twitching.

"Please, call me Dario." He smiled. "Both of you. I believe we'll be seeing more of each other and Heir-Lord Eribifax is such a mouthful."

"Very well." The Duke nodded. "You may call me Yanvian; I'm sure DeMaksim agrees to our informality. I wish to be kept fully informed of events, and based on my memories of your father, I look forward to our future association. You're welcome here at any time."

"Thank you." Dario sighed. "I'll do my best to meet your expectations."

"I'll break out the whisky-nectar then, shall I?" DeMaksim reached for ornate glassware.

Their acceptance had relief sweeping through Dario in a tidal wave. Now he just had to convince Zhulija.

CHAPTER FIVE

ZHULIJA

"What do you mean you had a meeting with Heir-Lord Dario Eribifax? Where and when?" Zhulija glared at her father. "I can't imagine any scenario where you'd chance meet an Unseelie lord."

"No chance meeting." DeMaksim swirled his glass of whisky-nectar. "He came here."

"*You* were there?" Zhulija's anger simmered.

Her brother shrugged. "You know Father and I work jointly running the estate." He sipped from his glass. "I don't do that from my bedroom."

"Lord Eribifax told the gate guards he had an appointment with me." Duke Yanvian smiled. "I admired his effrontery and acknowledged the appointment because we needed to talk about your assault whilst in his care."

"He was angry about it." DeMaksim whistled. "His hair lit up like a firestorm and his growling raised hairs on the back of my neck." He rubbed his nape. "You should've seen him." He shook his head, lips stretched into an admiring smile. "A worthy foe."

Zhulija's finger stabbed the air. "You're right, DeMaksim, I should've seen him." The finger swung. "Why wasn't I called to the meeting, Father?"

Duke Yanvian flexed a hand, palm upward. "I'm your father. It's my duty to care for you."

"And as your older brother ..." DeMaksim saluted her. "Between Father and I, we had you covered."

She ignored her brother. "How old am I, Father?"

"Twenty-eight." His brow wrinkled. "Why?"

"We're adults at 25, yes?"

His frown eased. "Yes, of course, but you're a fae-female, dependent on me and ..."

"Father, I'm no child." She bared her teeth. "If you cut me off financially, I could support myself through my art career. I continue to live here because I love and respect my family and don't see a need to move out." Her scowl flicked between them. "Yet it's clear neither of you consider me an adult worthy of respect. You're talking about me like I'm a thing instead of a person."

"Hey!" DeMaksim frowned.

She rounded on him. "Did you suggest I be asked to the meeting?"

"No." He backed up at Zhulija's incendiary glare. "Sorry."

Duke Yanvian spread his hands. "Zhulija, I simply accepted his apologies on your behalf and agreed to his offer of reparations. Although those are yet to be determined."

Zhulija gasped. "You accepted his apologies on my behalf? What part of me being a full-aged adult did you miss?"

"Well, none." Her father smiled, yet his eyes were hawk sharp.

"Don't try to play me, Father!" Betrayal tasted like bitter ash.

"I think you're being a bit dramatic, Zhulija." His smile turned toffee brittle.

"That's very condescending, Father!" Her hiss did justice to a kettle on the hob. "Let me show you how dramatic I can be." Her hands tensed into claws as she reached for a goblet of whisky-nectar to drown him in.

Her father put one hand up. "I thought I was acting in your best interests, Zhulija."

The nasty taste became a vile tide sweeping across her tongue to choke in her throat. "I don't see it that way!" Zhulija flung the goblet contents at him. Around the room, everything loose shot into the air, swirling and hovering. Pens, papers, tumblers from a desk. A carafe, napkins, a salver from the table. The avalanche of items hurtled at Duke Yanvian and De Maksim in the wake of the thrown goblet.

Duke Yanvian's eyes widened. "Demon spit! I thought avalanche abilities had been bred out!"

DeMaksim's jaw dropped. "What's going on?"

The cloud of disparate items rained forcefully onto the two fae-males.

"Ouch! Zhu, cut it out!" De Maksim crouched to avoid a tray.

"Zhulija! Stop this at once!" Duke Yanvian roared, batting at paper confetti. Both men raised their hands in self-defence, twisting and shrinking as they tried to avoid the barrage.

"I have no idea where that came from, but I'm according you the respect you've shown me!" Zhulija's voice echoed from all corners of the room; issuing from glass shards as a tinkle, from metal as a tinny screech, from paper as a sibilant hiss, from pens as a spatter of sparkling multi-coloured inks, which shaped her words in the air to glow like a display of fireflies. Gathering herself, Zhulija reined in the power she was startled to discover crouching white-hot inside her body, dropped her hands and glared at her father and brother.

DeMaksim sprawled on the floor, legs outstretched, propped up by arms rigid behind him. His face bore a few cuts and streaks of blood spotted his clothes. Duke Yanvian crouched nearby, similarly bedecked with cuts and specks of blood. They gaped at her like startled deer.

She swallowed, staring down at her hands, searching for traces of the power which had surged from them.

"Holy snapping swamp turtles!" Treymeron crowed from above them. "What in thunder was that, Zhu?"

Raising startled eyes, she saw Trey, her mother and all of her sisters leaning over the second-floor balcony.

"I d-don't know."

"Oh goodness!" Her mother's hands flew to her cheeks. "I haven't seen a display of avalanche power since my great-great-grandmother passed."

"That's all you can say?" Duke Yanvian's mouth thinned. "After Zhulija attacked us?"

"Serves you both right." The Duchess Azura wrinkled her nose. "She had cause. You were out of line excluding her from the meeting. Even Lord Eribifax should have requested her presence."

"Lord Eribifax did the right thing coming to see Father." DeMaksim wiped at a blood spot.

Snarling, Zhulija levitated a tray to thump into the back of his head. He fell forward to smack his face on one upraised knee. "Swofgtrh!" He cursed as fresh blood spattered.

"I deserved to be part of it, you misogynistic prig!" Zhulija's rage simmered. "Father, in future, I wish to be consulted about anything that relates to me. Are we clear?"

He was nodding when a knock sounded and the door opened to frame their major-domo, Entanglit. He offered Zhulija a tray containing a bouquet of flowers accompanied by a card. "From Heir-Lord Dario Eribifax for you, Lady Zhulija."

She snatched the card and read: "Pretty flowers for a pretty Lady. A small token of my apology. Dario." His signature was an elegant swirl. "Pretty flowers for a pretty lady! He sends me this banal, toad-eating smarm?" Her screech caused the debris of her 'avalanche' to stir in rustling threat.

Entanglit's eyes bugged at this unusual response to what he considered a respectable floral offering.

Zhulija flung up her hands; DeMaksim ducked. "I'm battered and bruised. I was treated like some sort of criminal. My hard work has been smashed into shrapnel and he sends bloody flowers as if I'm a pampered layabout? I'll show him flowers! Give them here!"

Mute, arms outstretched, Entanglit proffered the tray.

"Wait, Zhulija!" Duke Yanvian struggled to his feet. "Flowers are a tradition—"

He stopped at her furious glare.

"Flowers are meaningless. A gesture made by a coward who can't even be bothered to speak to me in person. We'll see about that!" Rage a living thing, Zhulija snatched up the bouquet and departed in a whirlwind of airborne wreckage.

Blazing ire helped Zhulija overlook the bruised soreness of her body; enough for her wings to carry her across the Rubicon River into Unseelie territory for the second day running. The Eribifax guards raised a hand in greeting as she approached, but she didn't stop. Zhulija aimed for the Eribifax welcome garden, touched down and surged along the path. Stones from the rock garden flanking the walk swirled up around her like an honour guard. Stopping on the veranda, she flexed her claws and sent the airborne rocks careening into the imposing front doors. Clatter! Bang! Thump!

As soon as the rain of rocks stopped, the door swung open to reveal the head of Suitilay the butler. His wary expression altered to startlement as he beheld Zhulija. His mouth opened.

Zhulija wasted no time. "You tell that damned haughty lord and master of yours that he can take his useless flowers and shove them where …"

The door was wrenched wide to showcase the fascinated features of Lord Dario Eribifax. "Yes, Lady Zhulija? Where might I put the flowers that I thought were a good start to my reparations?"

"You think these stupid flowers are a suitable start to reparations I wasn't even consulted about?"

"I visited your father and I understand it's common to apologise with flowers."

"I was attacked and my belongings smashed!" She vibrated with rage. "I'm not a simpering ninny to accept a pathetic bunch of common flowers to make up for such gross criminal behaviour." She slashed the bedraggled bouquet through the air. The absorbed fae-men contemplated the broken-stemmed, wilted flower heads, almost devoid of petals after their rough flight.

Dario offered a tentative smile. "Put like that, I can see I made a mistake."

"Oh, how clever you are!"

The smile on Dario's lips froze. Next to him, Suitilay winced.

"Perhaps—"

"You have the unmitigated gall to make arrangements with my father as though I'm a child, then send me flowers. You should have sent the gods-be-damned things to him! Of what use are they to me? All they do is send a message that you don't take me seriously because I'm female. You've disrespected me and murdered some poor innocent blossoms. It's like you're offering me a pat on the head. Shall I simper and flutter my lacy handkerchief?"

He tilted his head. "What—"

"You deserve to be strangled with the blasted handkerchief! I was the one assaulted! I'm the one whose belongings were destroyed! As an adult, I deserve to be the one whom you address with details of reparations. Not my father. Not my brother. Nothing is agreed upon until I say so. Got it?"

Dario didn't take his eyes off her. "You've made things crystal clear. In my defence, I just wanted to surprise you."

"Grrr." She ripped off one of the remaining flower heads and flung it at him. It hit his shin and dropped to lie on the veranda at his feet. "Surprise!"

He sighed. "I'm sorry that the flowers weren't to your taste. Any hints as to what might be?"

Hissing, Zhulija raised taloned fingers, swirled them and performed a flinging gesture. Flowers, leaves and twigs from the nearest garden beds rose in a cloud, circled, then pelted towards a startled Dario. He dove sideways to land supine on the decking, where he curled himself into a ball and cocooned himself in his wings.

With great presence of mind, Suitilay retreated inside and slammed the front door.

Shaking, Zhulija directed her avalanche of garden detritus towards Dario's altered position and watched in furious satisfaction as it pelted down on his foetal cocoon with stinging ferocity. She waited until her storm settled. Waited until Dario cautiously flipped his wings back to clear the debris. Waited until he sat up. Waited until his gaze tracked down his garden-bedecked lower limbs, across the veranda and down to where she stood at the base of the steps. Waited until he met her eyes.

That was the moment she flung the bedraggled remains of his pathetic bouquet with violent force. The few limp stalks hit him in the chest, then dropped to his lap as he sat gaping at her.

"I present you a bouquet of flowers in delighted thanks for your thoughtful consideration. I believe flowers do well in a vase of water." She'd altered her voice to a girlish coo.

He goggled, opened his mouth, closed it.

"You look like an ornamental goldfish." Zhulija wrinkled her nose at him before stalking away. Head high, body stiff with anger and pride, she rounded the corner of the track to the welcome garden, ensured she was out of his sight, then stopped. Sagged as her fulfilled anger died away, and pain from wrenched and bruised muscles reasserted itself. Flying here had been a fool's move, but anger had bolstered her, heating her insides like the small furnace in her studio. Now those feelings were ashes, and she didn't know where she'd find the strength to fly home again. On top of that, it dawned on her that, after her vengeful performance, she was stranded in Unseelie lands without friends.

She bared her fangs. "Bat turds!"

Tears flowed.

CHAPTER SIX

DARIO

"Wow." Brushing the garden refuse from himself, Dario shook his head. Zhulija had put him in his place ... hard. He grinned; his true mate had fangs and talons and wasn't afraid to use them. Things were looking up.

Behind him, the door opened. He turned, expecting Suitilay, but it was his mother, frowning at him.

"What was that about, Dario?"

He waved a hand. "Just getting to know each other."

"What an unusual dating style you have."

Dario glared. "I made a mistake." His lips twisted. "Lady Zhulija came over to point out that error."

"Really." Lady Catocala studied her son as if he had lost his wits. "It must have been an extreme mistake for her to undertake such a flight after yesterday's attack. You flew her home because of her injuries, didn't you?"

His eyes widened. "Blast and damn!" Whirling, he leapt off the veranda and sprinted down the path. The welcome garden came into view, appearing empty behind its hedged border. He slowed. She must have departed after all. Concerned for her welfare, unprepared for the volume of disappointment swamping him,

Dario stopped, hands on hips. He'd just decided to take wing when the sound of a sniffle reached his ears. Standing on tiptoe, he craned his neck.

There sat Zhulija on the smooth lawn, hugging her legs, her face buried between her knees. The peach-coloured fabric making up the panels of her skirt pooled around her, reminding him of a draping of loose flower petals. The glorious, black-splashed violet hair he wanted to stroke trailed in ringlets down her back, over a fitted, sleeveless cherry velvet bodice with matching boots. Her feet were drawn up like sentinels as she leaned into her cradled knees and rocked slightly.

With great deliberation, Dario scraped a foot through pebbles lying loose on the path. Zhulija stiffened. A lightning flash later, she'd rolled to her knees and used her hands to propel to her feet. When he strolled through the gap in the hedges constituting the gateway to the welcome garden, she faced him, arms akimbo.

"I deserved the treatment you just dished out." Zhulija stared, his blunt admittance appeared to disarm her. "I'm glad you understand. "Tears were drying on her cheeks, but she'd ignored them. Having just learned something important about his mate, Dario decided to do the same. "What reparations can I offer that you would be willing to accept, Zhulija?"

"Do you have any healing abilities?"

He shook his head. "I wish I did; I don't like that you're in pain." He might be able to sort something out though – there was a relative of Mycostat who did potions.

She sighed. "I can't craft things properly, or with any great speed, whilst I'm healing."

"Are you saying that you'd be willing to make items for Vinaya and Mycostat's wedding?"

"Perhaps the decorations for an Unseelie wedding would be an interesting addition to my achievement list." She shrugged, then winced. "Also, I wish to re-create my samples at some point."

Dario seized the olive branch. "What if I arranged for you to have an assistant?"

She cocked her head. "You'd do that?"

"If it'd help, it's a small thing I can do for both you and Vinaya." Dario watched as she tapped the toe of one cherry velvet boot on the grass. The movement fluttered the petals of her skirt. He allowed his gaze to wander up her shapely hips to the front-laced bodice caressing her waist, before it widened to curve around her bosom. Higher, the creamy honey of her skin appeared lickable, her elegant neck waiting to be nibbled upon, her lips … pursed with disapproval. His eyes shot up to meet hers, the violet orbs were shooting daggers. He essayed a weak smile.

Zhulija's hands went to her hips. "I. Am. Not. Your. Dinner."

He swallowed. Tried to look contrite. "Sorry." He wasn't. She was a delicious vision he would remember in his dreams later. "We've agreed you'd accept an assistant. What else?"

"I will need some supplies."

"Just tell me what you want and I will organise it." Did he sound too eager?

"A moment while I think." Her eyes became unfocused, she brought her hands up and used the fingers of one to count points off on the digits of the other. Her lips moved, words falling soft as floating gossamer. "Pretty sands for the tinted glass, wax for candles, gold and copper for filigree work, tiny coloured feathers …" Her hands dropped; she looked towards him again. "I'll need to work out my list and get it back to you. That will be the first thing I do in the morning. Please ensure that my assistant arrives ready to start at half an hourglass past dawn."

He bowed, entranced. "As you command, my Lady."

"I appreciate that you're willing to do this."

"My honour demands it, but it also pleases me."

"I thank you."

He wanted it clear between them. "You're accepting both my apologies and my reparations?"

"Alright, okay, yes!" She glared. "You really are persistent, aren't you?"

"Part of my delightful character."

She snorted. He watched her glance around, hated when her bearing changed from crisp command to a droop.

"May I fly you home once more?"

Zhulija considered him. "As part of the reparation?"

"Pfft." He flicked dismissive fingers. "More like common courtesy. Proper reparation is yet to come."

Her lips pressed together. "Now why does that sound ominous?"

Dario dusted a leaf from his hip. "I have no idea."

She contemplated whatever was behind him, not meeting his gaze. "I imagine you've worked out I'm too sore to fly."

He thought her pride adorable, but knew better than to tell her. "Don't worry, it'll just appear as if I'm ensuring your safe passage through Unseelie territory after yesterday's imbroglio."

Zhulija brightened. "Of course!"

Dario smiled, a hackle easing, widening his lips. Any Unseelie fae would recognise his repeated actions as marking his territory. So primitive. He couldn't wait for Zhulija's reaction when she found that the Unseelie were much more rough-hewn than the Seelie fae she was accustomed to.

CHAPTER SEVEN

ZHULIJA

*C*radling her mug of mint tea, Zhulija walked through the meditation garden as she made her way to the studio. The fountain splashed in the early morning light, a constant pacifying murmur. She passed the twins, Tindresse and Janeska, as they performed the graceful twirl of their exercise routine, raising her mug in salute as she progressed along the stepping stones in the path of enlightenment. Reaching the little rock shrine at the end of the path, she laid a leaf as her daily offering, before sidling around the shrine to pass under Old Lady Willow and onto the first bridge in the water garden. The ponds were all shallow and bedecked with lily pads and she admired the various colours of the lilies in bloom as she crossed the series of connecting bridges linking the sections of gravel paths. Beyond the water garden, the rambling roses of the cottage garden spread over the pergola, framing beds of hollyhock, foxglove, catmint, delphinium, phlox, peonies and cosmos, amongst others. Zhulija loved how they grew in a carefully cultivated wilderness of scented beauty.

Zhulija often winged her way over the top of all the gardens, but the passage through was a calming, energising ritual with frequent inspiration for her muse and today she felt in need of being soothed. This second day since her assault, the pain of her injuries was at an excruciating high; bruises blossoming in abstract purple flowers on her skin. Flying would've added to the agony and the stroll was loosening her sleep-stiffened muscles.

When her gazebo studio appeared against its forest backdrop, Zhulija was ready to meet Lord Eribifax's promised assistant and begin the planning of their work activities. Nobody waited on the steps. She frowned. Reliability was important, something she would emphasise to Lord Dario the next time she saw him.

Like right now.

Her mouth fell open as Lord Dario Eribifax turned from the top level of the veranda, where he'd been peering through the reinforced windows of her studio, and waved.

"A fine morning, Lady Zhulija."

Her heart rate increased. "Why are you here?"

"I said I'd arrange your assistant." He spread his arms. "Here I am."

"You're my assistant? What do you know about artwork?"

He shrugged. "Probably not a lot, but I'm a fast learner and very good at organisation."

She scrunched her nose. "Organisation of what?"

"Supplies, for a start." He beamed, beckoning high over her shoulder.

Completely puzzled, she turned. Hovering nearby were sixteen fae-males, each carrying large tubs emblazoned with the words 'Bollidee's Garden Supplies'. She must have been deep in thought to have not seen them sooner.

The leading fae-male winged closer. "Good morning, Lord Eribifax, where do you want the sand?"

"Sand?" Was that breathless squeak her voice?

"Just here, thanks." Smiling, Dario gestured to the ground at the base of the steps.

"Right you are."

A cascade of garden sand was delivered. The next fae-male added the contents of his tub, followed by another.

Zhulija watched in growing horror. "What is this sand for?"

"Glass making!" Dario raised his hands wide and high. "I thought I'd get a head start and surprise you. I arranged it with the gate guards." He waggled his fingers, grinning as he waited for her approval.

The contents of the last tub rained down upon the veranda, showering both of them with a strong and steady stream of grit. It saturated Zhulija's hair, trickled down her neck and struck her face in stinging particles. She couldn't see Dario, but she could hear him spitting and cursing.

"Oops! Sorry about that – a handle broke! Thanks for the order, Lord Eribifax."

By the time the air was clear enough to see, the deliverymen were gone.

"By Old Lady Willow!" Zhulija spat sand out of her mouth and contemplated her tea mug. It was now overflowing with tea-saturated sand. Her gaze swept the mess of sand cocooning them shin deep on the veranda, touched on the larger sand dune below, then met the crestfallen eyes of Dario.

He grimaced. "Sorry, that didn't turn out as I planned. It was going well before the last tub."

"You think so?"

"You don't sound pleased."

"I'm still coming to grips with all this sand, not to mention being covered with it." She gritted her teeth; particles of sand crunched and rolled. Working her tongue, she spat again, her anger rising.

"I didn't know there would be quite this much – it'll last you a while."

"Oh yes, it will. Forever, in fact."

A frown twisted his face. "What do you mean?"

Zhulija swiped more gritty grains from her mouth. "I mean that I don't use this type of sand – it's far too coarse. I've no use for it, so even forever is too short a time."

Dario's mouth fell open. He looked carefully around, taking in all of the mounded sand. "You – you don't use this sort of sand?"

"No."

"Oh." He took another look. "Not at all?" One hand covered his mouth.

She could see he was beginning to understand. "Not at all."

He bowed his head, turning aside. His shoulders shook.

Her anger gave way to uneasiness; surely he wasn't crying? "Dario? Are you alright?"

"Nnnh!" His snort echoed off the glass windows. Seconds later, he was roaring with laughter, hands dropping to his knees to support his unsteady frame.

"I don't think it's funny!" Zhulija's temper rekindled. "Look at this thrice-damned mess! It's all over us."

He pointed at her, seemed about to say something but a fresh paroxysm of mirth doubled him over.

"I hate sand in my clothes!" she hissed.

"No use!" He was howling like a fire-wolf.

Craning her neck at the sound of wings, Zhulija saw what she expected to see. Flying low above the trees, two gate guards, her father and both of her brothers burst into view in response to the estate breeching alarm.

"Zhulija, are you okay?" Duke Yanvian called as he landed. "Who attacked you?"

She clenched her fists. "My new assistant, Lord Dario, arranged for a blasted order of scum-sucking sand!"

"Sand?" DeMaksim back-winged. "Are you planning a new garden?"

"No, damn it!" She swallowed, drew a breath. "He ordered sand so that I – we – could make glass. He said he'd explained things to the gate guards."

Treymeron scratched his head. "Never seen you use any sand like this before."

She glared. "That's because I don't."

"Why is Lord Dario your assistant?" Her father was tapping fingers against his thigh.

"I didn't know he was until this morning."

The Duke switched his gaze. "Dario?"

He was sitting in their sand pit. "I couldn't find anybody on short notice."

Not laughing now, are you? Zhulija's satisfaction was short lived as more sand trickled down her back.

Her father gestured. "Whose idea was it to, ah ... wear the sand?"

Dario's mouth twisted. "The handle of a sand tub broke."

DeMaksim chuckled. "So, you received a delivery of sand you don't use, ordered by an assistant you didn't know you had, and it was dropped all over you by mistake."

Zhulija's glare drilled holes. "I knew I was getting an assistant!"

Duke Yanvian rubbed his mouth. "You just didn't know who." There came a snigger from one of the guards at the back of the group.

Zhulija seethed while the males exchanged loaded glances.

"Oh, this is the best!" Trey crowed. "I'd love to have seen the sand storm falling on you!" Seconds later, all men succumbed to glee. The two guards were holding each other up as they laughed.

It was the last straw for Zhulija, the reins on her rage broke. A tornado of sand shot into the air from around her, spinning out to sting everybody. Laughter switched to protest.

"Hey!"

"Zhu, stop."

"Zhulija! Cut this out right now!"

Leaving the flying sand to its own business, she marched into the forest and returned to the house for a shower. A vigorous application of soap, a cloth, and a cascade of warm water later left Zhulija clean and refreshed with not a grain of sand in sight.

～

Late morning found Zhulija inside her studio assessing supplies and making notes. Knocking interrupted her. She emerged from her store room to find a very sheepish Dario with his face pressed to the glass. Crossing to the door, she unsnapped the lock and slid it open.

"Yes?" She crossed her arms, wincing as the action pulled at the pain in her shoulder.

His smile was lop-sided, his hair a gorgeously contrived mess. "May I come in, Zhulija?"

She frowned. Why'd he have the gall to look so yummy while she struggled with injury and annoyance?

"I've brought lunch." He held up a basket.

"Any tea?"

He looked hopeful. "A thermos full."

With a huff, she relented. "Lunch and tea sound wonderful. Come in." As he passed her, Zhulija saw that he was wearing DeMaksim's clothes. "You've had a shower."

He cast her a speaking glance. "There was a lot of sand in unmentionable places."

Her face burned. "So I discovered."

Sighing, he placed the basket on her design table. "I'm sorry about that. I thought I was being helpful."

She flung her hands wide. "I understand, but Dario, it would've been better if you'd asked what was needed."

"It was meant to be a surprise."

"You certainly achieved that."

He winced. "But not in a good way." He shook his head. "You must be cursing my family for everything we've put you through. I can't say, or be, sorry enough."

She softened. "Let's sit and share what you've brought."

"Wait." He delved in his pocket. "I meant to give you this first thing, but, well … sand." He thrust a corked bottle at her. "It's a herbal healing elixir. I got it from Mycostat's mother – she's a potion maker."

Zhulija accepted the bottle but eyed it doubtfully. "She doesn't even know me. Why would she send me a healing potion?"

"Because Vinaya, Mycostat and I asked. Vinaya actually begged – she's set on having you make decorations for their wedding and Rympala will be Vinaya's mother-in-law." He opened his hands, palm up. "It will help you, Zhulija, I promise."

Concerns allayed, Zhulija uncorked the bottle and poured its contents into a glass Dario produced out of the lunch basket. A pleasantly herbal scent assailed Zhulija's nostrils as she raised the glass for a cautious sip of the thick, dark green liquid. She enjoyed the taste, hoping it worked to heal equally as well, and drank until the glass was empty.

"Here." Dario handed her a plate with a large slice of buttered nut bread, two hard-boiled eggs, some cheese and several straw-berries. A mug filled with steaming tea was set in front of her before Dario settled into another chair and tucked into his own plate of food.

"What sort of sand do you use for your glass making?" He sipped from his mug.

"Oh, I use very fine river sand. I collect it from the Rubicon myself." Zhulija chewed on nut bread before swallowing. "I visit a number of sites because there are different coloured sands. Some-times I dye the colour into it myself, but only if I have to. The colours Vinaya chose I already have."

Dario grimaced. "I've only myself to blame for that stuff up."

She pointed a strawberry at him. "Plus, Father, DeMaksim and Trey will all be gunning for me when I go back to the house for dinner."

He shook his head. "Don't worry, they'll leave you alone."

She blinked. "That's delusional. Yesterday I pelted them with ornaments and today it was a storm of sand. They won't be happy."

His smile was devilish. "Maybe not, but we all deserved it. I told them they'd have to go through me to get to you."

"Oh!"

He winked. "Can't let any more harm come to my favourite wedding designer, now can I?"

Zhulija's smile was weak. "No, no, of course not." His favourite wedding designer – the term sounded friendly and business-like.

"How's your lunch?" His lips stretched into the smile of a business-like friend.

"Just dandy." The food soured in her stomach as she experienced an epiphany. She didn't want a friendly business-like smile from Dario – she wanted to be the object of a white-hot, panty-melting smile.

She wanted him, full stop.

CHAPTER EIGHT

DARIO

*T*he sun was high when Dario arrived for their second workday. Later than he'd planned, but Eribifax Estate business neither disappeared nor completed itself. Entering through her open studio door, Dario went looking for Zhulija, surprised to find that the further he progressed, the more space he discovered. Of Zhulija herself, there was no sign. He spied more rooms opening off the main one, a lofty ceiling and ... was that a second level?

Scratching his head, he checked the distant door. He was in a gazebo. He knew he was. Scanning the place with mage-sight showed him the shimmer of plum-splat, the magical colour that accompanied enchantment casting. He whistled. An enchantment this large was unusual – the Duke either loved his daughter very much or had a pet leprechaun. Maybe both. Well, she wasn't here, but with an open door, she couldn't be far. He re-traced his steps, searching as he went.

Finally spying a note on Zhulija's desk addressed to him, Dario opened and read it. *Collecting things in the forest. Won't be long. Make yourself a cuppa.*

He decided to wait until Zhulija returned so they could enjoy a cuppa together. In the meantime, he'd observed several baskets of very twiggy branches. Time to make himself useful. He began to break the wood up and stack it in the fireplace. When the grate contained enough kindling for a fire, he filled the wood box next to the fireplace with more. By the time Zhulija returned, he was very pleased with his efforts.

"Good morning. I've got the tea mugs ready." Dario grinned at Zhulija. As he committed her windswept hair and prettily flushed cheeks to memory, a yearning to kiss her filled him. He restrained himself, knowing it was too soon.

Her return smile was akin to a blossom reaching for the sun. "There you are, Dario." She carried another basket of twiggy branches.

"Good, you have more work for me." He rubbed his hands together. "Although there's plenty of kindling from those other baskets that you left here."

She frowned. "Kindling? What?" She walked her basket to the work table, looking bewildered. "Where are the other baskets of twig trees?"

He nodded. "That's what I'm talking about. I saw you'd collected fodder for the fire, so I broke it all up to save you the trouble." He indicated the loaded fireplace and overflowing wood box.

Zhulija stared hard, swallowed and sank into the nearest chair. "Y-you broke them all up for the fire?"

"Yep!" Dario beamed.

She dropped her forehead into her palm. "They were the basis for the feather trees Vinaya has selected for part of her wedding decorations. I spent all morning looking for just the right-shaped pieces."

"Oh." Dario's smile faded. "Sorry."

Her smile was weak. "Never mind. Plenty more in the forest. I'll just go back and get other pieces."

"I'll come with you. Two of us will get it done faster, right?"

"Right."

He followed her, feeling like an idiot. Several hours later, he was an exhausted idiot. The pieces were required to look like little trees with lots of evenly spaced branches. Many of his finds were rejected because the branchlets weren't similar in size, shape and colour. By the time they'd collected enough for the wedding order, Dario had found only one that was acceptable to Zhulija. They'd walked around in circles, back and forth through the forest, in their relentless hunt for the damned bits of wood. Who knew selecting twig trees could be so difficult?

Day three was warm and sunny with gusts of wind. Dario was delayed by a messenger from his queen, requesting a full account of the attack on Zhulija. His queen being unhappy about the violation of her promise of safe conduct for Zhulija was no surprise, nor was the knowledge that she wanted detailed facts to concoct a punishment befitting the crime. Brax would suffer. The knowledge supplied Dario huge satisfaction; it served the sod right. Aware Queen Maerovana would send a dispatch to her Seelie royal counterpart, explaining her word was still trustworthy, his response was very detailed. Even though they were cousins, Queen Dianathke would draw as much enjoyment from seeing Queen Maerovana squirm as possible, and every ounce of humiliation Queen Maerovana endured, she'd take threefold from Brax's hide.

Climbing the steps to the closed studio door, Dario looked through the window to ensure Zhulija was inside. She was bent over a table sorting items into piles, so after a brief knock, he slid the door aside. "Good morning, Zhulija."

The wind chose that moment to whoosh into the studio with frolicsome glee, whirling fluffy bits off her table into a dust devil.

Zhulija flung herself over the table. "Quick! Close the door!"

Mouth agape, Dario stared at an eddying storm of feathers. Pretty, tiny, bright-coloured feathers. They spun everywhere in a crazy swirl, a lighter-than-air blizzard, with Zhulija stuck in the middle. Gulping, Dario slammed the sliding door. In his haste, he tore it from its door-track and barely stopped it from crashing to the floor. Gripping with both hands, wiggling and juggling, he finally got the sliding panel back onto its runners. Only then could he close it. With sinking heart, he turned, knowing he'd worked too slow.

"By Old Lady Willow, Dario!" Zhulija stood, arms akimbo as she glared at him. "The feathers are everywhere."

He sighed. "My apologies, although I don't see how I could have done anything to stop that from happening."

"You could have waited until I told you to enter." She was scowling.

"Yesterday, you said I could knock and walk in. I did. What more do you want?"

"For my assistant – that's you, I believe – to get here on time?"

He refused to be side-tracked by his admiration of her fierce spirit. "I'd love to be at your beck and call, Zhu, but I do have other demands requiring my attention. I'm doing the best I can. Now, let's re-gather the feathers. With both of us separating them into whatever piles you want, it won't take long to get them organised."

"My feather tree is awful!" Dario threw his hands in the air. Feathers fluttered in wild spirals of fluff. One stuck to his bottom lip; he sputtered and swiped at it. He glared as Zhulija fought a smile.

"It's repairable."

Thrusting hands into pockets, Dario angled away to find himself scowling at a series of glass statues arranged on one of the myriad shelves in Zhulija's studio. Frozen in their intricate poses, the statues ignored him. The figures of a male and female dancing were captured in sweeping, swirling elegance. Each pair blown in a different colour glass, the couples showcased stages of the dance as they flowed, dipped and twirled. Eyes moving down the line of dancers, Dario felt awe seep through him. He recognised the dance from the arrangement of line, shape, flow and colour in Zhulija's work. So beautifully crafted they appeared to be moving.

"You've created them dancing the Rhynfallia."

"Oh, you recognise the Rhynfallia?"

He nodded. "Hard not to with romantics in the family. Vinaya and Mycostat didn't plan a Valentine's Day wedding by accident." He flicked a glance at his pathetic tree.

Her fingers twitched at feathers – here straightening, there adding more string. "I imagine they're going to dance the Rhynfallia at their wedding then? Do they know if they are 'true mates'?"

Turning back to her glass-work, he bent, studying one of the statues in detail. "No, they chose each other normally, but when they perform the Rhynfallia in full, they might find they are. Vinaya would be ecstatic. Doesn't matter that falling in love can occur without 'true mate' recognition."

"It's what most fae want. Probably because they see a true mating as a certain thing." Zhulija tilted her head. "I've always wondered how Valentine and his mate Rhynfallia knew what dance moves to make, way back then."

"Maybe she invented it." He shrugged. "It is named after her."

"Yes." Scissors snipped behind him. "We know, now, that dancing the Rhynfallia reveals 'true mates' to each other and the completion of it will bind their souls if they are. It's even been said performing the Rhynfallia is like a game of chance – is your partner your mate, or just another dance partner?"

Dario grimaced. "I've heard some men label it entrapment. Caught whether they want to be or not."

"They have a choice." Zhulija's voice was tart. "Nobody forces them to partake of the dance. Besides, if they end up mated, it's their true mate. Why would they have issue with finding their beloved? Doesn't everyone yearn to find the fate-chosen, other half of their soul?"

"You'd think so." Dario craned to follow the flow of radiance highlighting the next set of dancers. "Maybe men just don't like admitting to being romantics. I know I don't." He twisted so that he could see both her and the statues, comparing her innate grace to that same quality in her work.

"Not very macho, you mean?" She turned the tree to a different area and added another feather.

"Many men won't admit to feelings." He grunted. "Whatever the reason, lots of people still dance at least part of the Rhynfallia. Can't find yourself mated if you don't finish the dance, no matter who your partner is."

"And, at some point, mates still have to do the traditional exchange of blood, the public claiming amongst witnesses, and the acceptance marking, fated or not." Zhulija laughed. "Still, it's hard to avoid dancing the Rhynfallia since it's played at every ball, and everyone adores it. I've seen same-sex pairs dancing it more than once."

"So have I." He grinned. "Some of those same-sex pairs find themselves mated too. We both know it's not because they can't find a partner of the opposite sex."

"That's true." She nodded. "Is that your way of telling me you prefer men to women?"

He choked as he met her gaze. "Mab's tits no! Whatever gave you that idea?"

She giggled. "Nothing. It was fun watching your reaction."

"Well, I like women. A lot." His gaze swept over her. "Lately, there's one particular woman who's piqued my interest." He took a step closer.

Zhulija moved around the table and pushed the feather tree he'd been working on towards him. "Ta-da! Your tree looks great now – it only needed a little more attention to detail." She flipped a hand palm up at the arrangement of twigs and feathers, smiling at him.

"Thank you for rescuing it." Dario wasn't sure if she was concentrating deeply or ignoring his advance. He studied her, noting the flags of colour darkening her creamy caramel complexion. Not unaware of him then. "You're having to do that a lot. I'm not much of an assistant, am I?" He placed the tree on the desk and folded his arms.

"Don't be put off, you're doing marvellous." Zhulija smiled encouragingly.

"Oh come on." He snorted. "First, there was the sand fiasco. Then I broke up all of the twig trees you'd painstakingly collected and put them into the fire pit because I thought that they were kindling."

Her smile was bright. "We collected more twig trees."

"After that, I opened the door and let the wind in while you were sorting feathers." He wrinkled his nose. "I'm sure I still have a feather stuck in one nostril."

She laughed. "The look of horror on your face was funny."

"On *my* face?" He shook his head. "I think you mean on yours. Seeing you fling yourself over the table far too late to stop the flight of the feathers was a sight to behold."

"Oh yeah? What about you, ripping the door off and struggling to get it back on its runners?"

Dario chuckled. "In that case, I'd say we both win the ridiculous crown." His smile faded. "I'm hindering you, aren't I?"

"You just need practice, Dario. Besides, you're wonderful company, and it's been lovely getting to know you." Colour rising in her cheeks, Zhulija gestured to the pots of twiggy branches and the piles of shaped and coloured feathers. "Now come on, they won't make themselves."

"A pity. Damn tree things." Dario wiped his hand across his mouth to hide his ecstatic grin. She really, truly liked him. He wanted to leap for joy.

"What was that?"

He spoke louder. "Just saying they're pretty grand tree things."

"Let's hope Vinaya and Mycostat think so."

CHAPTER NINE

ZHULIJA

*D*awn streaked the horizon as Zhulija wiped perspiration from her brow and contemplated the table full of glass pieces resulting from her night's work. She was grateful her ability to magically manipulate heat enabled her to create in glass and metal. Maman claimed ancestral dragon blood – something Zhulija was sceptical of. Whatever the reason, she could generate extreme heat but no flame. She'd gravitated to working metal and glass at night because the fae of her inner circle were sleeping and safe from the intense temperatures needed to sculpt those materials. She was also less likely to be interrupted.

Turning one glass hanging pot between her fingers, she checked for trapped air bubbles, satisfied when there were none. Naturally, each piece had been checked before being annealed but she still preferred re-checking afterwards. The blown-glass balls were so pretty in the peachy colour that passed for rose gold. They only needed hanging strings before they were ready for storage on the wall-mounted rope harness.

Zhulija removed a reel of finger-width, lavender silk ribbon from a cupboard and laid it on the table. Attaching the triple hanging ribbon-cords would be Dario's job when he arrived. She yawned, rubbing her eyes. It was several hours before Dario's usual start time; she could indulge in a nap and dream of him – a gorgeous man she struggled to keep her eyes away from and couldn't wait to see again. Yawning again, Zhulija settled herself comfortably on her daybed and drifted off.

It seemed no time at all before someone shook her awake.

"Wakey, wakey, Zhu."

Armelle's voice impinged on her semi-conscious state. Zhulija cracked an eye open; all her sisters hung over her like Old Lady Willow's drooping branches.

"Maman guessed you were here when you didn't appear at breakfast."

"We thought we'd bring some."

"Breakfast, that is."

Sighing, Zhulija opened her other eye and summoned a smile. "Thanks, I'm starving."

She was tucking into a bowl of berries with cream when the door whooshed aside to frame Dario. Zhulija's mouth watered as he strode in, his gorgeously windswept hair adding to his bad boy appeal. His large, muscled form was encased in a grey tabard, black trousers and well-worn, calf-high, black leather boots.

He cast his cloak over the back of a chair. "Please tell me we aren't making more feather trees today, Zhu. I'm over them." Sighting her sisters, Dario skidded to a halt so fast Zhulija wondered if smoke was rising from his boot heels. He cocked an eyebrow. "Hello, ladies."

"Good morning." Four voices chorused like birds tweeting in the dawn.

Zhulija waved; her mouth was full of berries.

"Lovely day." His smile upgraded him from gorgeous to breath-taking. Zhulija was glad to be sitting down – he made her weak in the knees.

"Wow!" Janeska shook her head.

Lyssica sauntered towards Dario, a shark scenting blood. "I'm Lyssica." Her voice was a purr. "That's Armelle to your left and behind Zhu are our twins, Tindresse and Janeska. You must be Lord Dario Eribifax." Her smile gleaming, she tucked a loose strand of dark hair behind her ear. "Zhulija's our baby sister, you know." Her lashes fluttered.

Zhulija glared at her sisters whilst chewing a strawberry.

Dario bowed, his eyes flicking over them. "A pleasure to make your acquaintance, ladies." His gaze returned to Lyssica. "Something in your eye, Lady Lyssica?"

"Perhaps you could remove it?" Lyssica cooed, leaning closer.

Hand tightening on her spoon, Zhulija wondered whether cream curdled as quickly as her feelings. Lyssica was an accomplished flirt; the 'something in my eyes' routine was a patented move. Zhu's annoyance flared – after she'd warned her sisters away, they were here making trouble.

"My apologies, Lady Lyssica, but my fingers are thick and clumsy. One of your sisters is a better choice to poke around a vital organ like your eye."

Zhulija's spoon jerked in her bowl, flicking a blueberry into the air. Her smile blossomed as Dario swept around Lyssica, caught the errant blueberry and popped it into his mouth. "Yum." He winked. Behind him, Lyssica scowled at his back.

Resolve firming, Zhulija stood. "Thanks, Lyss, I might be the youngest, but you've missed the fact that I've grown up." She knew, right down to the soles of her fluffy slippers, that her sisters were visiting to satisfy their curiosity about Dario. Was the baby comment meant to put her in her place, or warn Dario away? If they thought she needed protection, they were way off track. Were they trying to show her Dario was fickle and fancy free?

Dario's hand wave encompassed the group. "Are you ladies here to work then?"

Armelle wrinkled her nose. "By Old Lady Willow, no."

"We came to check on Zhu after she pulled another all-nighter." Janeska patted Zhulija.

She jerked away. "Quit that! I'm not a pet."

Tindresse added more berries to Zhulija's bowl. "Eat these up – you need the energy."

Zhulija's glare cut like a dagger. "I can look after myself. We spoke about this a few nights ago – if you recall?"

Lyssica ignored her. "Do you work out every day, Lord Dario?" Voice dripping with admiration, she reached towards his chest. "You have amazing muscle definition."

"No." Face expressionless, he stepped sideways to avoid her fingers.

"Your colouring is wonderful." Armelle pouted her lips. "I've always adored red, black and silver grey together. I'm sure your wings are very pretty."

Dario's lips twisted into a sardonic grin. "Are my eyes sparkly silver too? Perhaps red to indicate lust, or anger?"

Lyssica barrelled on despite the acidic response. "Do you style your hair or is it naturally that wild?"

Tindresse clapped her hands. "It looks silky – may I touch?"

Dario folded his arms. "No."

Janeska took a step, but Zhulija dropped her bowl on the table and grabbed her sister's arm. She opened her mouth—

Dario's voice was splintering shards of ice. "Let's be clear, ladies. I'm not interested in spreading my wings to show off my colours, or in having my muscles stroked, and if anyone touches my hair, I usually break their fingers. I'm not here to socialise. I came to assist Zhulija with her crafting. You read me?"

"Oh, but Lord Eribifax—"

"Not clear then." He squared his stance as if preparing for a rough and tumble. "Listen up. I've no wish to offend, but none of you interest me apart from being Zhulija's sisters." His glare swept over them. "In that position, I'll accord you the respect that you accord me. Got it?"

Zhulija grimaced. "Alright, dear sisters, I've had sufficient to eat so please take the dishes back to the kitchen as you go. Thanks for thinking of me. Don't come back." She snatched up the carry bag, thrust her bowl and spoon inside, then swept across the room to hold it out.

Tindresse took it, her smile wry. "You're spoiling our fun, Zhu."

"No fun here. Take yourselves elsewhere, we've work to do." She met the eyes of each of her sisters, baring a warning fang. "Leave. Now."

"Fine." Lyssica shrugged, but a flush mantled her face and neck. "I'm sure we'll see you later, Lord Eribifax."

"See you at dinner tonight, Zhu." Armelle offered Dario a weak nod then followed Lyssica.

"Are you sure, Zhu?" Janeska cocked her head.

Zhulija's lips wrinkled, revealing both fangs. She hissed.

"Ookay." Janeska and Tindresse hastened past Dario.

The door shut with a crisp snick.

Dario raised his eyebrows. "Was that a test of some kind?"

"My sisters checking up on me. I apologise for their behaviour."

His expression remained neutral. "You wanted to see how committed I am, then?"

"I did not arrange that sisterly drama." Zhulija's brows drew together. "And, committed to what? Assisting with Vinaya and Mycostat's wedding pieces?"

His lips thinned. "The wedding pieces – yes, of course."

She nodded uncertainly – were they speaking of the same thing? "Well, we are on a time-line."

"So we are." His smile was harsh. "Is that why you worked all night?"

"Partly."

"The other part being that you don't trust me not to muck things up somehow?"

She shook her head. "No. Blowing glass is tricky, needs complete concentration and at night my family are asleep, so no interruptions."

Dario massaged the bridge of his nose. "No interruptions by me, you mean?"

"That's not what I'm saying." Zhulija rolled her eyes. "You know you're easy on the eyes, milord – another distraction I can't afford when blowing glass."

He brightened. "You feel uneasy around me – I understand that. You were attacked in my home, I orchestrated the sand fiasco, the branch disaster and the feather storm. Add my pathetic attempts at feather trees and you probably thought I was a sure bet to wreck the glass blowing somehow." He winked. "Me being such a distraction and all."

She ignored her blazing cheeks. "You're a distraction for any red-blooded fae-girl, but again, this had nothing to do with you being gorgeous and everything to do with the privacy I need for glass blowing."

He nodded. "Okay, but you're more to me than just a 'red-blooded fae-girl' and I'm the biggest distraction you'll ever have. You know that, don't you?"

Zhulija tipped her head to the side. "What in the name of the Queendom are you talking about?"

His lips twisted. "Fine, play innocent, but we both know the truth." He spun towards the door. "I need air." He strode out.

Anger bubbled to life – how dare he walk out on her without proper explanation! Bursting on to the veranda, she found Dario stalking to and fro, muttering to himself. "You stop right there!"

He whirled, eyes phasing through silver and black to crimson. "Give me a good reason."

Zhulija blinked. With deliberate steps, she closed their distance to tap a fingertip on his chest. "Listen, it's no lie that I blow glass at night, alone. You don't have to flatter and flirt with me – it makes me uncomfortable when it's not true."

"Flatter and flirt? You think I'm playing you?"

She waved a hand. "That business about attraction between us." She shrugged. "You and I both know you're handsome and I realise from the looks you've been dishing out lately that you find me good looking enough to notice – but you must have tonnes of far more suitable Unseelie ladies at your beck and call. I have no wish to be a curiosity for you to bed and set aside."

"A curiosity? You think this is a casual attraction?" He glowered. "You insult both of us. It's fortunate I know the truth between us."

Zhulija sighed. "We're back to that truth business again? I told you – my night work has nothing to do with lack of trust."

His lips flattened. "Wrong truth, Zhu. You're being deliberately obtuse. The one I'm talking about is something we both recognise on a gut level but you won't admit and I can't tell you without breaking fae-law."

"By Old Lady Willow's roots! This is bloody ridiculous. I've no idea what you're blathering about. Why can't you just get to the point?" She jerked on his tabard, digging her claws in, dragging him down until they were nose to nose. "Explain it to me, Dario. Now!"

The gust of his cold mirth bathed her. "As you command, darling!"

She had no time for breath, only shock, when his mouth sealed her own; his lips moving, deliberate, intent, delicious. Unable to resist, Zhulija pushed up to deepen the inexplicably wonderful contact. She thrilled as Dario's arms encircled her, dragging her hard against him. Mindless, she lifted her legs to wrap around his hips, locking them behind his back. He jerked against her, their fangs clashing, tongues twining, lips moving slickly. She writhed to get closer still, sliding her arms up his marvellous chest and about his neck. Her talons scraped his scalp, clutching at strands of silky mane. His wildly aroused growl reverberated inside their mouths. Zhulija lapped it up, revelled in him; sank into his flavour of sunny forest glades, the air after spring rain. He was as decadent as molten chocolate swirling on her tongue; she couldn't get enough. The taste, the sensations, his stroking, soaked into her parched soul, just as surely as their veins flowed blood …

Blood? Zhulija jerked her head back to stare at Dario. He panted, eyes kaleidoscopic with flaring patterns of argent, ruby and ebony flame. Her tongue touched her bottom lip, tasting the shared slick of blood as it blended deliciously in her mouth. She could feel her fangs throbbing, see Dario's, gleaming white behind his blood-painted lips.

"Y-you kissed me!" Her tongue snaked out, slid over wet lips before flicking across to share his, another taste of nirvana between them.

"Just as you kissed me." He grinned, eyes burning. "Everything about you says you yearn to do it again." His voice dropped to a growl. "As do I."

She swallowed, unable to deny it. "I need to think."

He shook his head. "Tut-tut. Thinking is over-rated, Zhu." His fore-claw stroked her cheek. "With thought, we talk ourselves out of so many truths. Feel this thing between us; feel, as well as think. Add our emotions, the way we've touched, the flavour and mix it well. Recognise that it's not simple lust. Therein lies your answer – our answer." His lips caressed her trembling mouth again, before sliding to kiss her cheek, eyebrow, forehead. Bewilderment flooded as he set her away, holding her tight just until her shaky legs supported her. "If you trust me as you say, you'll work it out, sweet Zhu. I can't be any clearer without breaking fae-law." He backed a few paces, meeting her stunned gaze with those wild, kaleidoscoping eyes before arcing his striated wings and arrowing skywards.

~

Clutching her hair with clawed fingers, Zhulija sensed wildness rising. Shivering, she stared until Dario faded from view, then screamed to the empty sky.

He, a known ladies' man, had rejected her sisters, threatened to break their fingers, gotten annoyed at what he called 'her games', revealed hurt feelings at perceived slights, become angered at what he saw as lack of trust, and yet, kissed her into yearning craziness …

Why?

What did he want from her?

He talked in riddles. What must she recognise? How did you combine emotion, touch and flavour with thought? Logic and sensation were oil and water.

If he was right and she had the answers, he must already know them …

She couldn't ask him, but others had visited her studio.

Fanning her wings, Zhulija sped homewards to face her sisters on the breaking waves of her wrath.

Ignoring the guards angling towards her from their gate duty in response to her screams, Zhulija aimed for the French doors and burst in from the gardens. Gathered for lunch, her family whirled from the buffet at her volcanic eruption into the room. Her father, brothers, even her mother had assumed defensive stances in front of the girls; they relaxed upon recognising Zhulija.

Her mother stepped forward with arms outstretched. "Zhu! Is something wrong?"

Ignoring her mother, she aimed a claw-point at her sisters. "What did he mean?"

"Ah, what did he mean by what, Zhu?" Armelle spoke softly as if sensing something was not right.

"By what he did? By what he said?"

Armelle cocked her head. "You mean in rejecting Lyss's advances?"

Side-tracked, Zhulija's frozen gaze swung to Lyssica. Her mouth wrinkled in a snarl. "You attempted to seduce him."

Lyssica backed up. "I wouldn't have really. I was protecting you, Zhu!"

"You all tried to steal him!"

Janeska raised her hands, palms out. "No, we were testing him, Zhu, seeing how committed he is to you."

"He thinks I don't trust him."

"Do you?" Her mother.

The savagery swirling inside her hesitated; she tilted her head. "Yes!"

Duke Yanvian pointed. "Why is your face covered in blood? Is it yours?"

"He – I – we ..." She swallowed, brought fingers to her lips. "We kissed. Our fangs cut, the blood belongs to both of us."

"What?" Duke Yanvian let loose a roar of outrage. "That Unseelie jackal had the gall to kiss you and exchange blood? I'll have his guts for boot laces! I'll rip that pretty boy hair out strand by strand! I'll—"

"You won't touch him!" The guttural thunder of Zhulija's voice was emphasised by an airborne cloud of objects, rattling into her personal halo. She raised claws sparking purple, her hair billowing as if in a gale.

"No, Zhulija!" Her father froze. "No, no, you're absolutely right. I won't touch him. My apologies for threatening him. No one in this room will touch him without your permission. He is safe and, and, welcome in our home."

The words settled, felt right. She glared at her siblings; they all looked away. Whispered words in her mother's calming tones drifted her way.

"There's no threat, Zhu. Stand down, relax and feel safe knowing that Dario is yours alone."

The breath caught in Zhulija's throat. "Mine? Dario is mine?" Items dropped as Zhulija's palpable shock undermined her use of power.

"Of course he is, sweeting." Duchesse Azura smiled warmly. "That's what this is about. The intense attraction, the newly revealed power, the exchange of blood between you – you're mate-claiming Dario Eribifax. And he, you."

"Mate-claiming." Zhulija let the phrase roll through her. "Oh! We're true mates! That's what he couldn't tell me." She caught her mother in a wide-eyed stare. "It's against fae-law; he must think I'm a total idiot."

Duchesse Azura opened her arms. "I doubt it, sweetling. He'll be waiting for you."

Gulping, Zhulija ran into that soft, warm, tried-and-true embrace and snuggled in.

"Well, thank the gods!" Duke Yanvian sagged. "But an Unseelie son-in-law." His groan was heart-felt. "DeMaksim, some whisky-nectar, please?"

"Can I have some too?" Treymeron sidled up to his brother. "I'm overcome with angst."

DeMaksim set out a row of tiny glasses. "Push off, Trey."

But after he poured, he handed everyone a restorative glass.

CHAPTER TEN

DARIO

*D*ario tapped a pen on his desk-pad, concern eating him up inside. Another day over with no message from Zhulija. He'd given her an ultimatum – painted himself into a corner. Why hadn't she answered? He flung the pen to the desk, splattering ink across the open document.

"Mab's tits!" Snatching up a sponge, he dabbed at the mess.

"Really, Dario." His mother frowned from the doorway. "Your face is black enough to give the staff nightmares."

"Sorry." He wasn't. He wanted to rip the document into tiny pieces and scatter them; swear until his voice deserted him; fling black shadows until people understood that he was the nightmare.

"Excuse me, your Ladyship." Mycostat eased around Lady Catocala and plunked a glass into Dario's hand. "Try this."

Dario drained the shot of whisky-nectar like spring water. Mycostat refilled it from the bottle he held, watching Dario scull it again.

"Dario! Go easy on that." His mother caned her way into the office. "We don't need you drunk as well as lovesick and sense scattered." She relieved him of the sponge and wiped up the ink.

Mycostat snorted. "Relax, your Ladyship; it takes a lot to get Dario mellow. I've never seen him drunk."

"Nor will you." His father, haunted by memories of the war, had coped by drowning himself in alcohol and had been killed while too drunk to defend himself. A mistake Dario had vowed never to make. He deliberately ignored the rest of the accusations his mother voiced.

Vinaya sailed in. "I've made us a huge pile of sandwiches." She plunked a small plate containing a lettuce leaf and four points of a single sandwich on to the smeared pages. They all stared at the pathetic offering.

"Naya, that wouldn't feed a rabbit." Mycostat rubbed Vinaya's back. "Nice thought though."

A breath of laughter escaped Dario. "I'd hate to see your version of small if you consider that paltry offering a huge variety."

Suitilay arrived, pushing a cart containing two much larger trays of sandwiches and a third tray of cake. The trolley's second shelf bore the tea urn, cups and fixings.

It was Vinaya's turn to laugh. "Ha! Tricked you. There is a lot of sandwiches. I just allowed Suitilay to bring them."

"At least he can be trusted to have *your* back." Dario couldn't resist the verbal jab.

Suitilay looked down his nose. "I fail to see how leaving myself open to a rain of garden refuse could further my unquestionable allegiance to the family. It was aimed at you, my Lord, and you deserved it."

"Touché!" Dario's right hand flipped palm up. Everyone laughed.

With a bow, Suitilay withdrew, leaving them to the picnic.

The butler returned a half hour later. "My Lord Eribifax, you have visitors."

"Show them in." Dario was afraid to hope.

Suitilay pushed the door wide. "Your guests, Heir-Lord DeMaksim Aphiski, Lady Lyssica Aphiski and Lord Treymeron Aphiski." Both fae-males carried crates and Lady Lyssica had a basket athwart one arm.

For a moment, Dario stared in frozen shock. Then his wits and manners reasserted and he introduced everyone.

Lady Catocala nodded. "Charmed to meet more of the Duke and Duchess Papillion's brood."

"I'm sure the pleasure is ours." DeMaksim bowed over the crate he held.

"Can we put these down now?" Treymeron asked. "This member of the brood is tired."

"Mycostat, would you please help Lord Treymeron?" Dario moved to assist DeMaksim.

"Sure." Mycostat put down half a sandwich and crossed to help with the load.

Treymeron smiled across the top of the crate. "So you're the groom whose wedding these baubles are for."

"Baubles?" Vinaya clasped her hands. "Oh wow! Lady Zhulija came through. That's wonderful, isn't it, Mycostat?"

"Absolutely." Mycostat watched Vinaya prying at the crate lids.

"Like this." Treymeron showed them how the covers unlatched.

"I've a reel of lavender silk ribbon for the baubles – they'll be suspended from the ceiling," Lady Lyssica said to Vinaya. "That was one of Lord Dario's planned jobs, but he didn't finish."

"Oh, that's alright." Vinaya smiled. "I can do that. I'd love to. You won't mind missing out on that, will you, Dario?" She aimed a cheeky grin at him, but it faded as she saw the way Dario and DeMaksim were eyeballing one another.

Locked in his staring match with DeMaksim, Dario's eyes burned as they begin kaleidoscoping.

"If you hurt her, I'll kill you," DeMaksim lisped around enlarged fangs.

"I plan to love her, not harm her." The red heat flashed from Dario's eyes and up into his hair. He growled.

"Wow." DeMaksim chuckled. Did his skin look scaly? "You have it as bad as she does. Wonderful."

A growl vibrated from Dario. "Where is Zhulija? Why are you here instead?"

"She's finishing some items." DeMaksim's fangs had reverted to fae-normal, just small top ones. "Without your assistance, she needs to work harder to complete the wedding paraphernalia."

Dario frowned. "That's a weak excuse. If she doesn't want—"

"Zhu needs time to process, think and make her decisions, and if you're smart, you'll allow her to have it. She's an emotional whirlwind. Father threatened violence against you, which had her setting up to attack him. He backed down, apologised and promised no harm would come to you."

"She defended me? With that tornado of stuff she conjures?"

DeMaksim's grin was beatific. "It was brilliant, although terrifying when it happened. Maman calls it avalanche power – an old, recessive family trait."

"I know how he feels." Dario shook his head. "Poor Duke Yanvian – I wonder if he needed to change his underwear?" The two fae-males locked eyes in mutual understanding and burst into laughter. Dario sighed. "Okay, I'll wait for a sign from Zhu."

After a searching glance, DeMaksim nodded. "She said to tell you there's a gift."

"A gift?"

"It's Valentine advent five-day. I believe that she has a few more planned." DeMaksim was grinning. "Lyssica, give him the first gift."

Lyssica's hand appeared over DeMaksim's shoulder, holding out a mid-size rectangular box wrapped in gold foil and tied with a bow. "From Zhu."

Accepting the gift, Dario moved to his desk, unwrapping the package with slow, shaking fingers. She hadn't given up on him.

"Hurry up Dario! I want to see." Vinaya was dancing in anticipation.

"It's my present." Dario held his breath as he drew off the lid and pushed aside the tissue paper. Inside lay a gold filigree pen. Jaw dropping, he stared. Was it? He lifted his scarred left hand to compare ... yes, the pattern was identical. He laughed so hard he fell off the chair.

His guests weren't allowed to leave until he'd wrapped up the Eribifax heirloom pen as Zhulija's return gift. By then, they were all laughing.

The next day, DeMaksim and Trey were accompanied by Armelle. Their crates held the feather trees, which were unpacked to the accompaniment of laughter as Dario related how he had chopped the first branches up for firewood.

His Valentine advent gift from Zhulija was a smaller version of the round glass bauble vase that had been made for the upcoming wedding of Vinaya and Mycostat. It contained sand and a small bouquet of flowers. He understood the reference to the ill-fated posy he had sent, which she had re-delivered in pieces, accompanied by part of his garden. His Zhulija was certainly getting her pound of flesh. He loved it.

Suitilay smirked at seeing the gift in pride of place on Dario's desk. "I believe Lady Zhulija's a fitting match for you, my Lord."

Smiling, Dario continued to stare at the little vase. This time, he'd prepared his return gift in advance. He refused to tell Armelle that a trio of rare burgundy blood roses, a gift fit for his queen, nestled inside the gift box. He wondered what Zhulija would make of it.

What she made of that Valentine's Day lead-up gift was her own version. A single burgundy blood rose in blown glass.

Dario's hand trembled as he held it. Zhulija had probably stayed up, just for him, the previous night making it.

"Wow, Dario." Vinaya sounded awed. "That is so-o beautiful!" She paused in unpacking her filigree flower holders to admire it.

It was a work of art revealing the hand of love in its glistening perfection. He laid it reverently back in its silken nest and arranged the box where he could see the rose at will.

Which was often.

The return gift he entrusted to the basket held by Janeska was a box containing an antique key with a silk bow through its top loop. There was nothing to tell Zhulija what it was for. If she accepted him as her mate, he'd show her the beautiful gazebo remodelled to mirror her studio. No discussion had occurred between them about a mating, never mind living arrangements if their mating came to pass. In truth, he'd no idea what Zhu thought. Aware of their significance to each other, he'd come to terms with the possibility of spending time in both realms – that was doable while he was only Heir-Lord. After seeking advice from his mother, he'd advised Queen Maerovana of events, pointed out ramifications, even dared to make suggestions. Her answer, the response of a dangerous fae-woman who was a law unto herself, had yet to come.

Day four's wedding finery proved to be filigree baskets with brackets for place cards, cushioned by sponge leaves in DeMaksim and Treymeron's crates.

Tindresse carried a basket containing several packages layered in soft leafy coverings. She presented the basket to Dario. "Today's Valentine advent gift from Zhu, your lordship."

Dario unwrapped the series of glass statues he'd last seen gracing a shelf in Zhulija's studio – the beautiful frozen couple in their intricate poses, dancing the sweeping, whirling Rhynfallia. Each set was a different hue of glass, while showcasing progressions of the dance as the pair glided, angled and spun. In admiring the procession of dancers, Dario experienced a repetition of the awe that had swept him at his first viewing. He recognised anew the dance from the exquisite positioning of line, form and colour in Zhulija's artwork.

"By Queen Mab!" Lady Catocala caned closer for a better look. "Those statues are superb, Dario."

"Lady Zhulija is a true artist." Vinaya crouched for a closer view.

"I didn't think she'd ever give those away." DeMaksim was shaking his head.

"Hope you've got something good, Lord D." Trey grinned. "Hard to counter these."

In answer, Dario handed over a large envelope.

"A card?" Trey mocked. "That the best you can do?"

But Mycostat whistled. "That's no card – that's an invitation to Queen Maerovana's birthday ball tomorrow night. She was born on Valentine's Day eve and holds a ball every year; she handpicks all the guests. It's said to be amazing."

"You were invited, Dario?" Lady Catocala looked pleased. "What an honour. Where is she holding it this year?"

"On Garadenya Island in the Rubiconia River." Dario was relieved. His queen had replied to his missive with a pile of invitations. "We're all going, Mother. Me, you, Vinaya and Mycostat." As she gaped, he turned to DeMaksim. "I also have invitations for your entire family." He produced a second envelope. The Aphiski contingent were equally startled.

Lady Catocala's hand firmed on her cane. "Well, that explains why it's on the river isle – neutral territory."

"Yes, a deliberate choice." Dario winnowed a hand through his hair. "Queen Maerovana's cover note said she wants to meet the lady whose safe pass was violated and all parties concerned."

Tindresse's hands flew to her mouth. "Oh goodness, everyone will need a special outfit!" She chivvied her brothers out the door as fast as possible.

"She's right. We've no time to waste! Come on, Vinaya." Lady Catocala grasped her daughter's arm and dragged her off.

Mycostat poured himself some whisky-nectar and topped up Dario's glass. "Mab's tits. It always comes back to clothes." His expression was morose. "They'll be after us next."

"We both have new outfits for your wedding, in two days' time." Dario saluted his future brother-in-law. "Can't get more perfect than that."

Mycostat sighed. "Dario, that's genius, but the women won't let us get away with it."

Dario pursed his lips. "I'd better ask Suitilay to request the presence of the tailor with some outfits then."

"Now? You think he'd come here now?"

"He'll come." Dario's smile revealed his sharp fangs. "We have an understanding."

CHAPTER ELEVEN

ZHULIJA

Garadenya Isle blazed with light. Zhulija marvelled at how night's darkness fled before the false daylight provided by myriads of festive lanterns strung from every tree and pole. She tapped one foot to the strains of music drifting out of the fortress as she stood in the receiving line with the rest of her family. The music was entwined with infectious sounds of gaiety, announcing the progress of Queen Maerovana's Valentine birthday ball to anyone with ears. Waiting for the queen's major-domo to announce them, Zhulija smoothed shaky hands down the pearl-sprinkled, fitted lace bodice of her dark cherry gown and fluffed the tulle layers frothing over the satin underskirt. Black lace gloves without fingertips encased her hands, a perfect frame for the sparkling silver points of her polished burgundy finger-nails. Even her extruded claws had been painted burgundy and silver in case a claws-out event occurred. Flexing her fingers as the line moved forward, Zhulija kept eyes on her parents and simply alternated her black cherry satin boots in their wake. Around Zhulija, her sisters were twittering with excitement, ignoring their brothers who brought up the rear of their family cavalcade.

"The Duke and Duchesse of Papillion, Heir-Lord DeMaksim

Aphiski, Lady Lyssica Aphiski, Lady Janeska Aphiski, Lady Tindresse Aphiski, Lord Treymeron Aphiski, Lady Armelle Aphiski and Lady Zhulija Aphiski." Listing them in birth order, the major-domo's sonorous voice rolled like an ebbing tide over the clamorous sea of people in the great hall. He spoke quietly to her father, who nodded before escorting her mother downstairs to the main floor where they stopped. DeMaksim's hand under her elbow helped Zhulija's confidence as the siblings followed. A tall female-fae with lemon-speckled, dark teal hair approached in a swirl of marigold satin to speak to their parents. Zhulija could hear nothing of her speech over the revelry.

"With that gorgeous colouring she has to be from the Zygaeniday family." DeMaksim's smile was predatory.

Zhulija kept her voice as confidential as her brother's. "You'll have time to socialise later."

He grinned. "Looking forward to it." A squeeze of his fingers urged her to follow their parents and the Zygaeniday lady. The Aphiskis were guided between bouncing brownies, gyrating gnomes, undulating dark elves, dour dwarves with gnarly beards and cackling pointy-hatted witches. Zhulija was startled when a puca winked its velvety black eye and rattled its chains in her direction. Occasionally, a light elf shone amidst the ocean of dark fae.

Resplendent in their finery, enthroned side by side on a dais, were the two queens of the fae world: Seelie Queen Dianathke, and her Unseelie counterpart, Queen Maerovana. Their proximity revealed the familial heritage of their shared great-grandfather, King Oberon. It was apparent in blue eyes and the similar cast of honey-toned features, but where Queen Maerovana was a busty golden blonde, Queen Dianathke had rich chocolate hair and a lissom build. No one disputed the loveliness of either queen, or their reputations of ruling with a firm hand backed by strong individual magics.

At this first meeting, Zhulija had envisioned the Unseelie queen would be dark featured, like the reputation of the Unseelie fae, and the Seelie queen would be correspondingly fair and pale. At her thought, both queens focused on her, smirking. Seconds later, Queen Dianathke's chocolate hair became ash blonde while Queen Maerovana's hair turned midnight blue. Zhulija froze.

"Tut, tut, Lady Zhulija." Queen Dianathke retained her lazy smile, but Queen Maerovana's gaze was eagle intense.

"Apologies for not guarding my public thoughts, your majesties." Zhulija dropped into a deep curtsy. "I meant no disrespect."

The Seelie queen continued to smile. "That, we could also tell, Lady Zhulija."

Duke Yanvian frowned. "Forgive—"

Queen Dianathke shook her head. "Not now, Yanvian. We will talk later."

Tight of mouth, Zhulija's father bowed, but his eyes flashed Zhulija a warning as he stepped back.

Flowing to her feet, Queen Maerovana glided down from the dais to confront Zhulija. Her well-built shape was more buxom up close, whilst her hair continued to shade from midnight through all shades of blue, to blonde and back in a continuous pattern of colour and light. Bright blue eyes were dagger sharp with the force of her power and presence. Zhulija swallowed under the queen's pin-point focus.

"So, you're the girl causing me to hold my birthday ball in this out of the way place." Her voice rang bell-like across the great hall causing a silence that spread like ripples in a pond, until the entire hall was cocooned in quiet expectation.

Zhulija swallowed. "I beg your majesty's pardon, but I'm not sure what sort of impact I had on the situation. I had no idea where your birthday ball was being held until I received an invitation yesterday."

The queen nodded. "Oh yes, I'm sure that's true, but Dia and I have been hearing lots about you."

"You have?" Zhulija wasn't certain whether to be alarmed or not. When Queen Maerovana began to circle, Zhulija turned with her, attempting to maintain eye contact. She wasn't certain she wanted the Unseelie queen behind her. A tinkle of laughter came from Queen Dianathke, still seated on her dais throne.

"When a request came from the Eribifax family for a safe pass into Unseelie territory for the youngest daughter of a Seelie duke, I was naturally curious. I asked Dia what she knew about this Lady Zhulija Aphiski, who was suddenly of high interest to some of my people. Dia explained that you were an artist who makes wedding decorations as a side business. I had thought an artist who must make trinkets to survive couldn't be a very good artist, but then Dia showed me a few, acquired pieces of your work. They're better than good, they're beautiful. Tell me why a gifted artist feels the need to make wedding paraphernalia?" Queen Maerovana stopped moving to stand side on to both the dais and the bulk of the great hall.

Zhulija shrugged. "It helps my thought processes. Wedding pieces were amongst my first efforts; now I've made most of the items often enough that I can still think and plan my major artworks without being idle. I suppose you could say it's creative doodling."

"Interesting." Queen Maerovana pursed her lips. "Once I saw your artwork and understood why the Eribifax family wanted your visit, I decided to grant the pass. I didn't expect you to be any trouble, but that was proved a fallacy when my pass, my word of protection, was dishonoured by a footman on the Eribifax Estate." She shook her head. "I was pleased Heir-Lord Eribifax sent him to me, not easy for him under the circumstances, but I had a lovely time questioning the treasonous creature." She shook her head sadly. "Where do these crazies get their ideas? Have you ever wondered, Lady Zhulija?"

"No, your majesty. I haven't come up against anyone like that before."

"Fortunate girl in your sheltered life." The Unseelie queen made a moue. "I have been unlucky enough to meet more than my fair share. This particular one was most upset that you had escaped him and very angry that you had burned Heir-Lord Eribifax. He believed you should pay." She snorted. "Pay for being Seelie instead of Unseelie? He ignored our common heritage. Foolishness." Queen Maerovana's fanged smile was viciously pleased. "He has discovered, the hard way, my lack of tolerance for fools."

Uncertain of the conversation's direction, Zhulija stayed silent.

"I was fascinated when I heard Lord Dario still bore the scar from your burn instead of having it healed, as he easily could have done." Queen Maerovana cocked her head. "Did you find it strange, Lady Zhulija?"

"I haven't given it much thought, Your Majesty." Zhulija curled her fingernails into her palms, wondering where Dario was. "I am unaware of the Eribifax family's skills."

"Of course you are." Queen Maerovana nodded. "I contacted Lady Catocala for details and her response intrigued me enough to continue our correspondence. Imagine my surprise when I discovered one of my justifiably feared, and trusted, Unseelie lords had offered his own services as reparation for the wrongs done to a duke's youngest daughter. Few people would understand why he was doing the reparations with his own hands, but Dia and I were convinced there could only be one reason."

"My Queen, Queen Dianathke, I greet you both." The sound of Dario's voice was wonderful. He swept a deep bow. "If you would allow the indulgence, I believe it's my turn to speak with Lady Zhulija."

Zhulija looked across to the stunningly handsome fae-male who she had finally understood was her mate. As usual, his shoulder-length tricoloured hair was angled in multiple directions and he wore the Eribifax family colours. His form-fitting trousers were charcoal leather, snugged into calf-high black boots, while his sleeveless silver tabard, fitted over a crimson silk shirt, was complemented by a low-waisted black belt, from which hung two short hip swords. His dark grey eyes were full of warmth; his smile stroked her skin.

Zhulija reached for Dario's hand and ran her fingers across the filigree scarring. "Why didn't you get this burn healed?"

"It bothers you, Zhu?"

"I've never before hurt someone that way."

"I should hope not!" Dario grinned. "You marked me, as true mates do. I was yours on the first day we met, even if you considered it to be only a self-protective act. You mate-claimed me; there was no way I was going to have the mark of my beloved removed."

Zhulija's palms flew to her cheeks. "You knew? Way back then?"

"I did, though I confess I thought a gentle Seelie lady couldn't be strong enough for the Unseelie Beast." He reached, clasped a hand and drew it from her face. "You soon proved me wrong." Keeping her hand in his, Dario dropped to one knee. "I'd like to tell you I'm very much in love with you, Zhulija Juniper Aphiski. Would you be willing to fulfil our mating and share your life with me?"

"Oh! Oh, yes, Dario. I'm in love with you. Of course I will." Zhulija swept close to Dario and pulled him up for a kiss. A delicious meshing of lips to rediscover his flavour of sunny forest glades tangled with the aftermath of spring rain. His arms snugged around her, their mouths briefly parting, before reconnecting to lick deeper into their kiss. Zhulija was so wrapped up in Dario, she forgot where they were.

"Ahem!" Queen Maerovana tapped both of their arms. "True mates are always a delight. Too bad there aren't more such unequivocal unions. Tell me, Dario, have you marked Lady Zhulija in return? Not yet? What about the sharing of blood? You've completed that? Good. You've been marked, but she hasn't, you've shared blood, you've accepted each other here, in public, as true mates, In that case, I believe it's time for dancing."

"Dancing? Now?" Zhulija, eyes only for Dario, identified the indignant voice of her younger brother.

"Yes, now, young Lord Treymeron Aphiski. Now is the perfect

moment." Queen Maerovana turned to wave at the musicians. "Play the Rhynfallia for Lord Dario and Lady Zhulija."

Zhulija stared up at Dario, wondering how she could be so lucky.

His smile was a thing of love and wonder. "The Rhynfallia – you will dance it with me, won't you, darling?"

"I'd be delighted." She swung into his arms for the first few steps as the music cascaded around them. Separating to fingertips, gazes connected, they moved in graceful arcs to the lilting melody before parting to retreat in a smooth but intricate foot pattern, to circle one another in lithe fluidity, swirling to the music with a supple agility that elicited "wows" from the riveted watchers. As they danced, dipped, twirled and spun, Dario and Zhulija had eyes for no one but each other while they performed the ancient fae mating ritual, which was only ever a total success for true mates.

The music rose to a glorious crescendo as Zhulija came once more into Dario's arms for the closing rhythms of the ceremonial dance. The moves of the Rhynfallia routine were so finely struc-tured that a finishing point could be predicted once the later stages were completed. Zhulija and Dario flowed through their final elegant glide into the penultimate moment, where their wings spread in arcs of brilliant colour. Spinning Zhulija back over one arm, Dario bent to kiss her. His hand on her neck eased up to caress the sweep of her hair before flowing back to stroke her nearest wing.

Overflowing with love and joy, Zhulija felt a heat trailing over her brow, following Dario's palm to her wing, then spreading across from one wing to the other. He was marking her in his own way, just as she had done. "How did you mark me?"

His eyes brimmed with love. "I've put a dash of my family's crimson colour in your hair and altered the cobalt markings of your wings to also be crimson."

"Lovely." Her mind began to buzz, as if someone spoke just outside the correct wavelength. Unconcerned, Zhulija drew Dario down for another kiss, just as a hand landed on each of her shoulders. Startled, she drew back; Dario had also jerked, but his grip on her tightened as they both sought the cause of the unwelcome interruption.

Queen Dianathke stood to one side, a hand on each of them, with Queen Maerovana on their other side in the same position. The two queens spoke as one, their combined voices rolling like thunder through the great hall.

"I accept the true mating of Lady Zhulija and Lord Dario, and from this day forth, claim them both as my subjects. They have marked each other, exchanged ritual blood, declared their acceptance of each other as true mates and danced the Rhynfallia to its shared conclusion. They are one in our sight and our service."

The buzzing in Zhulija's mind crystallised into clarity as soon as the two queens finished the marriage declaration and fell silent. Her thoughts were invaded by a shout: *"Zhu's mine and I'm hers!"* She winced, followed the line of speech back to its source.

"Dario?"

"Zhulija? You can hear me!" Her mind rang with the power of his internal voice as Zhulija nodded. Dario hugged her tight.

Beside them, Zhulija saw the two queens share a satisfied smile.

CHAPTER TWELVE

DARIO

"*D*ario, can you believe the queens gifted us Garadenya Island?"

Zhulija and Dario stood in the turret's highest room overlooking the driveway. Said driveway and its flanking grounds hosted a chaotic spread of fae – dancing, laughing, screeching and yodelling at the moon. No one seemed to care who was Seelie and who was Unseelie.

"No, I didn't expect something as wonderful as that." Dario breathed in an exquisite lungful of honeysuckle and Zhulija. At the end of the driveway, the estate gates opened to the centre of the bridge across the River Rubiconia. Turning left led to Unseelie territory and right to Seelie lands. The queens' generosity, coupled with their joint claim of ownership of both Zhulija and himself, meant both of those directions led to home. They were no longer simply a Seelie lady and her Unseelie lord, they were both. "It comes at a price though."

"One we agreed upon." She turned her head to meet his eyes. "You don't regret becoming agents for the combined crown of the fae-lands? That we are the border force for both Seelie and Unseelie?"

"Regret it?" Dario shook his head. "Absolutely not. It was a brilliant manoeuvre. They've been unable to decide how to deal with this castle athwart the river on no-man's land for centuries. Our mating will help to bridge the cultural divide between the Seelie and Unseelie sects, making the term 'no-man's land' obsolete. As a group, our joint families make this region strong and none of us want to see any resumption of the inter-fae wars of 50 years ago. Our queens know we're loyal to the Linked Crowns because they saw inside our minds at the conclusion of our Rhynfallia."

As we did each other." Stretching, Zhulija pressed a kiss to Dario's lips. "Will you mind not inheriting the Eribifax Estate? Now it's been transferred to Vinaya and Mycostat after Lady Catocala?"

He sighed. "I cannot deny I love that estate; I grew up there, it was my home and I will miss it. Just as you will miss the home where you grew up."

She tapped his nose. "What about the reparations I am owed?"

Dario flung his arms wide. "You have me; I'm your reparation."

"That's all I get?" Zhulija pouted.

His mouth dropped open, then closed with a snap as she dissolved into laughter.

"Cheeky little minx." He was grinning.

"I'm releasing you from the debt."

Dario wrapped his arms around her again. "Zhu, my sweet, I'll happily spend the rest of my life ensuring you achieve appropriate reparations."

She frowned. "What's your idea of appropriate?"

"I'll let you know when we reach that point." He rubbed his thumb along her bottom lip. "But here, we won't have to buck years of tradition. It's exciting that as the first Duke and Duchesse of Garadenya, we can create our own traditions, find our own way."

"I like the sound of choosing our own path to the future. Shall we start now, beloved?" Looking at him from under her lashes, she licked his thumb, then sucked it into her mouth.

"What a delightful idea, my darling." He slipped his thumb free to taste her lips again. Moving on, he kissed her cheek, her eyelids, her brow; slowly ran his hands down her back to her waist and paused. "Have I told you how delectable you look tonight? I adore the way the top of this dress cups your breasts, then spreads into that puffy high and low skirt over your sexy heeled boots ... I want to peel the top down, flip the skirts up and have you lock those boots around me."

"Oh! Goodness. There's my beast." Zhulija's cheeks swamped with colour.

"You're blushing, sweetheart." He nibbled a soft kiss to the side of her neck, then hesitated. "Would I be wrong in thinking you innocent in the art of love and sex?"

"Not wrong at all. There was no one I was attracted to."

"Erm. Okay." Dario's throat rippled. "I can go slow, but ah, how slow would you like? What if I ... Do you know ... Perhaps I should explain ..." He floundered to a halt as she let out a happy trill of laughter.

"Oh Dario." Zhulija nuzzled his jaw. "I know how everything works; I just need a little practice."

Grinning, he opened his arms wide. "Here you go. I volunteer for practice." He choked when his novice mate flattened her hand against his erection and rubbed, feeling and shaping with a firm grip. He pushed into her grasp as pleasure flooded him. "Uh, wow. Perhaps we should move on to something else."

"Y-you don't like my touch there?" Zhulija caught her bottom lip under her fangs as she studied him from under her lashes.

"I like it too much, Zhu." His confession rewarded him with her sunny smile. "Continue and I would finish very quickly. I want us both fully engaged here."

"What do you suggest then?"

He reached for the buckle of his sword belt. "Let's work together undressing. Look how my belt releases." He re-clasped it and let Zhulija undo the tricky buckle before placing his sword belt carefully against the wall. He stripped off his tabard and tossed it, after her nimble fingers made quick work of the triple-grouped side strings. Shown the hidden ties of his shirt, Zhulija released them, allowing the shirt to gape as she patted his chest. Reaching around her, Dario grappled with the hooks of her gown. Becoming distracted when she rubbed her hands across his abs, stroked his nipples, then kissed and licked from one side of his chest to the other, he shivered.

She sighed. "Mmmm."

Growling, he clenched his hands in the fabric of her dress. "Wait." He was panting. "I don't want to rip this gorgeous outfit." She giggled, but stilled while he freed the gown. It slithered from her body to the floor, a dark cherry froth of lace, tulle and satin.

"By Queen Mab's … um, er …" Dario was riveted to the mouth-watering sight of his mate wearing her boots, tiny red lace under-wear and no bra.

Zhulija was cupping her bare breasts with a wicked grin. "No dead queens here, last time I looked. I believe these are my breasts, Dario, I hope they'll do instead." There was her cheeky, under-the-lashes glance again. He loved it.

"You're so beautiful you put the moon to shame – who needs Queen Mab?" He fitted his own fingers around her stunning breasts, thumbed the hardened nipples, before lowering his head to nuzzle, lick and suckle until she was gasping and mewling in his grasp. He dropped one hand to cup her sex, pushing at her under-wear until Zhulija helped him dispense with them. Separating her legs, Dario felt Zhulija arch upwards to meet the fingers he slid into the heated, luxurious wetness awaiting him.

"Dario, oh!" Writhing in his arms, she rubbed her breasts against his broad chest and moved around his massaging fingers. When her mouth flowered hot against his, their bodies snug, he took the opportunity to lower her to the soft velvet coverlet spread out and waiting. He crawled over her and his fingertips went back to working between Zhulija's outspread legs. Kissing her breasts again, he took turns drawing the tips into his hot mouth. She was shuddering in delight as his lips traced a smouldering path down her sweet body. Rimming her belly button with his tongue, tracing kisses over the line of one hip, he continued downward to the pearl centred above the entrance to her sex.

She went wild as he licked and sucked the hard little nub, his fingers still circling, dipping and massaging her inner passage. She bucked under him, then lifted her hips to grind against his marauding mouth and skilful hand. His tongue kept flicking and swirling until she exploded into a shivering, shaking, gasping paroxysm of pleasure. He continued to kiss and lick and love her through the aftershocks, until she stilled, eyes closed.

Rolling to one side, Dario finished removing his boots and trousers.

"Dario?" Zhulija stirred, opening one eye.

"Just taking the rest of my clothes off, darling." He returned, sliding up and over her body, taking pleasure in the friction of his chest against her swollen breasts. "Are you okay, my sweet Zhu?"

"Yes, let's do this; I need you, Dario."

Their mouths met, her tongue there to greet his. "With pleasure, my Zhu."

He rubbed his erection against the damp swollen folds between her legs, eased himself inside her gorgeously firm channel. Shivering at the marvellous sensations of tight, wet heat, he pushed forward and felt the gasp of breath explode from her mouth when her innocence gave way. Dario paused, deepening their kiss, sliding his hands up to play with her nipples and give her the time to adjust, even though it was torturous to stop so close to nirvana.

"This feels amazing, Dario."

Zhulija finally reached to cup his bottom and urge him on. Unable to stop himself, he thrust until his erection was totally swallowed and they both cried out in wordless delight.

"Are you okay, sweetheart? Any pain?"

"I'm fine, better than fine. More please."

Wasting no time, Dario pulled back then pushed forward again. Zhulija rose eagerly to meet him, tilting her hips so he slid even deeper. They gasped and Zhulija flexed the muscles of her sex around his erection, wiggling beneath him in playful experimentation. That wrecked Dario's control. His next thrust was faster, the pleasure escalating each time he drew away and plunged back to fill her. They rocked in a sea of overwhelming sensual enthusiasm, grappling to keep each other close, to love each other more, until Dario stiffened, feeling a roiling tsunami sizzle out from the base of his spine. He exploded in fierce thrusting pleasure, against her, inside her, surging to a completion he'd not expected in his wildest dreams. He felt Zhulija's muscles clamp tightly around him, before a low gasping cry left her lips and she joined him, shaking with her own release.

"Happy Valentine's Day, my darling." Dario leaned in to kiss Zhulija on the lips, just as Vinaya and Mycostat completed their wedding ceremony with a kiss. His sister and Mycostat were definitely in love, but they didn't have the 'true mate' connection that he and Zhulija had found. True matings were rare; everyone rejoiced when they did happen, but love matches were equally accepted, and Dario was happy for Vinaya and Mycostat. They'd still dance the Rhynfallia but they wouldn't be rewarded with the divine inner connection he and Zhu had found.

Zhulija cocked her head. "I am curious about one thing."

"Only one?" He waggled his eyebrows. "The world is full of curiosities." He bent, chuckling as she poked his ticklish ribs; something she'd discovered during the night. He'd found a few interesting erogenous zones on her body also.

"It's the gift of the key you gave me." She raised her own eyebrows. "What's it for?"

"Ah." He nodded. "Come, I'll show you." He escorted her from the rose garden, around the back of the Eribifax mansion and along a path between a pair of tall hedges. To one side of a small lake, a gazebo glistened. "Your key opens this replica of your gazebo studio. I had it constructed for your usage when you were here."

"You believed I would move here after our mating?"

He shrugged. "I wasn't sure. I knew we would have to work hard to cope with the Seelie/Unseelie aspect of our relationship, so I thought that we might alternate between here and either your father's property or somewhere of our own in the Seelie lands. I was going to discuss it with you in order to achieve mutually acceptable arrangements."

Her face softened with love for him. "Could you be any more perfect?"

Colour darkened his cheeks. "I'll do my best."

"Too bad my new studio is now in the wrong place." Her mouth drooped.

"You still need a studio." Dario grinned. "I'll have no trouble getting it transplanted to Garadenya Island, my love."

"Oh, yes!" Zhulija clapped her hands. "That's wonderful."

He cupped her chin in his palm. "Promise me one thing."

"And that would be?"

"We come from different worlds, so from time to time we will experience difficulties."

She nodded. "I can't argue with your logic."

"Promise me we will always talk things through, find answers we can both relate to."

"Yes, I agree to that." She tilted her head to kiss his fingers. "A wonderful idea, my Unseelie Beast."

"I pledge you the same, my Seelie Darling."

Her smile warmed his heart. He kissed her ravishing mouth until they were both panting.

She licked her lips. "I have an idea."

He eyed her, wondering how soon they could return home for more loving; he felt in a constant state of arousal around her. "Yes?"

Zhulija reached into the valley between her breasts and withdrew her key. "Let's go check out my gazebo. We can test how well the door locks." She winked at him. "From the inside."

He reached to run a finger along her bottom lip. "What a delightful idea."

"I thought so."

Grinning, Dario swept his mate up and settled her into his arms as he raced for the gazebo.

~ THE END ~

Thank you for reading Zhulija and Dario's story. I hope you enjoyed it. If you'd like to find out what happens next, then I recommend Cherith and DeMaksim's story!

Find it here:
Ancestors and Expectations

ACKNOWLEDGMENTS

With sincere and profuse thanks to my fellow authors, Leisl, Marnie and Sam, for their assistance, technical know how and continuous encouragement. You're all very wonderful to work with and I'm blessing my lucky stars to have been included in the group. The publication of our anthology, with my story included, is a dream I'd never expected to achieve – so glad to be proved wrong!

Tales from the Fae Court, Book Two

Ancestors and Expectations

What if the truth doesn't set you free?

BESTSELLING AUTHOR
HELLUCY HOWE

What if the truth doesn't set you free?

As eldest child, Seelie Lord DeMaksim Aphiski is expected to be the Papillion Duchy's heir. Until the day he breathes fire. Blue blazes, is the rumour of a Dracon in the family actually true? Needing answers, DeMaksim pursues a report of a draconian family connection into the threatening Dark Reaches, and suddenly his life takes wing.

Unseelie Undine-Eldwytch crossbreed, Cherith Beriaden has the soft core of a plant nurturer but the appearance of a soul-sucking killer. Wrenched away from her water-roses just to tail a spy, Cherith is even more annoyed when the dolt turns out to be gorgeous. River Goddess! Who knew she had a weakness for vazel eyes?

Unexpectedly bound together by a warped Unseelie monster, Cherith and DeMaksim are forced into an awkward partnership. If the monster still lived, she could snap the connection in seconds, but now they have to seek answers elsewhere. Hopefully by All Hallows' Eve. Forced to cuddle together at every rest period, freedom is top priority for both of them ... isn't it?

Read on for a sneak preview of Chapter One!

CHAPTER ONE

DEMAKSIM

A massive elderoak dominated the clearing, its characteristically drooping branches reaching for the sky, the thick, age-whorled bark a rough brown cloak. The sign – Elderoak Tavern – hung from one branch, squawking in every wind gust. Straightening his leather jacket, DeMaksim thrust the door open and strode inside. Conversation ceased. The curious stares of patrons elicited a crawl of goosebumps as he threaded his way to the bar encircling the tree's heartwood. Rolling his shoulders, he wished he could scrub his spine against bark to ease both the goosebumps and his aching wing muscles.

"Whaddya drinking?" A grey leathery-skinned monolith with a rock-solid build and a voice which rumbled like a grating slide of scree, shuffled from the shadows of the trunk's core.

DeMaksim cleared his throat. "Flamuisge, neat."

The flicker of the Rock-troll's beetling brows dislodged a sliver of crumbling shale to the counter top. "Hope yer gut's strong."

DeMaksim chuckled. "What food's on offer?"

One square thumb elevated. "Squirrel stew." A finger joined the thumb. "Two hunks of toasted rye-bread with berries." The second finger. "Vegies with green dip." A third finger. "Powdered lime-stone on gemstone chunks." Fourth finger. "Dwarf bread."

"Hmm." DeMaksim rubbed his chin. "The stew, thanks."

"Five coppers the lot."

Reaching into his waist pouch, DeMaksim eased the metal chips free, pushing them across the polished surface. He was impressed how quickly the troll's blunt, stony digits nimbly palmed the coins.

Stubby granite teeth glistening, the craggy behemoth filled a beaker from a keg, then plunked it in front of DeMaksim. "Grab a pew."

Holding his mug, DeMaksim crossed to an empty window booth; his moulded leather trousers slid easily along the wooden pew. Studying the panes of glass beside him, he decided the name 'window' was a misnomer – years of dripping sap covered any possible glass. Fortunately, the gloom was lightened by glow-bug wall sconces.

"May I sit with you, Sir Fae? I dislike drinking alone." A woman approached his table, her red-lipped smile afire with invitation. Coppery hair rustled as she swept it artfully behind her.

"Not buying." Set on his mission, DeMaksim was in no mood for pick-ups.

"I already have a drink." Her wide-lipped smile failed to reach her eyes as she produced a flask from her shoulder-bag and sat. "Are you from around here?"

"Thereabouts."

"Got any kinfolk?" She fingered the design etched on her flask.

"Why?" Her questions, especially to a Seelie this deep into Unseelie territory, raised hackles.

A hiss of laughter. "Just small talk."

The troll appeared, placing a wooden trencher in front of DeMaksim and a second, larger beaker of liquid. "Water's free."

"Thanks." The delicious aroma of the stew was its own adver-tisement. Fisting the spoon, DeMaksim dug in. Despite his hunger, he remained uncomfortably aware of the fidgeting woman across the table; of her intent gaze, the fingering of her flask, the rearrangement of the burgundy flower nestled in her hair, the trailing of her fingers down her neck, across her throat and down her right breast.

DeMaksim chewed, swallowed. "Not interested."

She frowned. "I'm trying to get to know you."

"I don't want you getting to know me." He spooned up more of the delicious stew.

Pouting, she tapped a finger on the wooden surface. "Just trying to be friendly."

He grimaced. "Take a hint lady – leave."

"Thraxarkzal!" Two dwarves lurched against the table; one with fists in his opponent's beard, jerking the long fibres. DeMaksim flinched as Mr Trapped Beard bit his antagonist's nose and yanked an ear.

"Bezeknazonite!"

"Durkitz!"

Rock-like grey arms yanked hoods tight around dwarfish throats as the Rock-troll bartender – ignoring choked cries – dragged the pair of brawlers to the door and ejected them.

DeMaksim spooned the last few bites of stew, chomping hard on something tough. Rewarded when it popped, he swallowed, grabbing a chunk of bread to drag through the gravy.

A sly smile widened the face opposite. "Good stew?" Lamplight glinted off small, curved fangs. "I thought Fae were herbivores?"

"Look for prey elsewhere."

Her purr was throaty. "I like you."

He tensed. "Go away." Something unpleasant roiled in his stomach; it heaved. Bile threatened. Recalling the tough thing that'd squelched in his mouth, DeMaksim's gaze narrowed on the smiling, over-friendly female fiddling with her hair blossom ... again. His lips tightened. "You seeded me."

Hasty fingers dragged red tendrils from her flower – the

further her hand stretched, the longer the strands became. Grinning, she cast the threads.

Snarling viciously, he flexed his dagger from its forearm sheath, slicing through the airborne strings. Shrieking pieces plummeted to the table, the strands writhing, blackened where he'd cut them.

"No!" Delicate, curving fangs morphed into vicious, hooked needles.

"Nageen!" DeMaksim vomited, continuing until a coiled pile of snake fell to the table-top. It raised a scaly, hissing head, but DeMaksim called forth a sheeting whoosh of flame, searing the rejected invader and the extra red tendril chunks he'd slashed. Those would've sealed a lesser Fae's fate.

Hissing like steam from a covered billy-tin, the Nageen's eyes slitted, barbed fangs protruding from her suddenly reptilian mouth. Her forked tongue flickered. "But you're just a Fae! Fire isn't possible!"

"Damnation take you!" Slamming fists on the table, DeMaksim spurt-flamed the seeding pod disguised under burgundy hair blossoms. It shrivelled to a blackened wisp.

Screaming, the Nageen abandoned all pretence. It transformed into a large, thick serpent and slithered hastily for the door. The doorbell clanged repeatedly, forced to open and shut for each coil of the reptilian body as she fought to escape. The repetitious sound echoed through the suddenly empty tavern.

DeMaksim retched again.

The Rock-troll appeared, carrying a wooden bucket and a fresh beaker of water which he shoved at DeMaksim. "Good job, Dracon." Using a cleaning cloth he swiped the table several times, rinsing and wringing the cloth between wipes. "She won't be back."

"You could've warned me." Scowling, DeMaksim dragged the back of his hand over his mouth.

The Rock-troll shrugged. "Mate, get real. Ye're in the Dark Reaches. Wasn't sure what she was until she started her play, anyway." His chuckle grated like stones. "Yer handled the rest right fine."

DeMaksim peered around. "Where'd everyone go?"

"Out the back door as soon as yer started flaming." The bartender considered him. "She's right, ye look Fae."

"I *am* Fae." DeMaksim snatched the water beaker, gargled and spat the befouled liquid onto the buckled curl of his plate, all the while holding the Rock-troll's wary gaze.

The bartender raised his hands, the cloth dripping down his upraised arm. "I offer no harm, I'm …"

"A united Queens' man. Their symbol's etched into your arm."

"Damn." The Rock-troll dropped his arms. "Shouldn't have rolled my sleeves up. Yer got a problem with it?"

"Blue blazing hells, no." DeMaksim's smile was wry. "I'm one too." He flipped the collar of his sleeveless jerkin aside, revealing the united Queen's symbol tattooed under his right collarbone.

"Okay then." The bartender nodded.

DeMaksim held his gaze. "Not that it matters, but I *am* Fae; with a few inherited extras."

"Ah, draconic bloodlines." The Rock-troll nodded sagely. "Hard to dilute traces of ordinary Dracons, never mind Primordial Elementals. Gotta name?"

"I'm Mak."

"Good to know, Mak, but I meant the Dracon. Do ye know which of them is yer ancestor?" One lichen brow raised waiting for an answer.

DeMaksim scratched his head. "How would I know if it was one of the Primordials?"

"How long ago was it?"

"Three centuries, give or take a few years."

"Oh?" The bartender resumed wiping the table. "And yer can still flame? Impressive." His hand swept away ash and molten shrapnel. "Need more clues. What'd yer say its name was?"

"I didn't."

"Do yer know?"

"If I did, how would *you* know whether it was a Primordial Elemental?"

The Rock-troll laughed, a rocky booming sound. "It's all in the name, Mak Fae-Dracon. Names are power and there weren't many Primordial Elementals. They came into being when the world was born, are made of the same stuff and will probably be here until the world ends. Or maybe they'll survive. If yer got one of those in yer ancestral line, I'm staying on yer good side. Ye get me?"

DeMaksim huffed a laugh. "Yeah."

"Mind if I ask what ye're doing in the Dark Reaches? Many of the wilder Unseelie Fae and malcontents from the Fae Wars skulk out here."

"Any Draconfolk?"

The monolith's brows arched. More shale shards crumbled down his body. "So! Ye're hunting?"

"Just information." DeMaksim shrugged. "I want to know who bequeathed us the draconic traits; some family members claim it a myth."

The Rock-troll's guffaw shook the table. "Yer flaming ability's no myth."

"Exactly." DeMaksim drank some water. "The idea consumes me; my evolving abilities have created a personal imperative. Queens Dianathke and Maerovana granted me rights to search the royal archives. That's where I found clues suggesting the Dark Reaches as a good place to seek answers."

Dropping the cleaning rag into the bucket, the bartender braced fists on hips. "It's also a good place to find trouble, young Fae lordling, serious trouble."

"Fae lordling?" DeMaksim frowned. "That's a huge assumption."

"Nah, yer dropped the royal names like rain on daisies." The Rock-troll rolled his eyes. "Dead giveaway. Ye're a Fae lordling alright. Out here, yer gotta watch yerself. Letting on yer know either queen can get yer killed."

"Look around you." Lifting the water beaker, DeMaksim

saluted the bartender. "I reckon I'm looking after myself right fine, Sir Troll who knows the Queens right well."

The Rock-troll's laughter rattled the sapped-in windows.

~

Want to find out what happens next?
Grab your copy here:
Ancestors and Expectations

OTHER TALES BY HELLUCY HOWE

~

The Fae Courts

A sweeping fantasy romance series filled with fae, gods, magic... and plenty of adventure!

A Perfectly Paranormal Anthologies

A collection of paranormal romance anthologies in conjunction with several other wonderful authors.

~

To find out more about any of these, visit my website:

www.hellucywrites.com

PART OF THE TRIBE

I love to hear from, and keep in touch with, fellow book worms! If you'd like to spend a little more time together, you can find me in the following places:

FACEBOOK

- A Perfectly Paranormal Anthologies Reader Group - Perfectly Paranormal Paramours

Or send me an email at - hellucywrites@gmail.com - I love hearing from readers and authors alike!

ABOUT THE AUTHOR

Meet Hellucy Howe, a Book Dragon who teethed on romantic fairy tales and went on to voraciously devour anything paranormal. Writing was also second nature but became something to do in secret when the stories of her young child mind were ridiculed. Homes were populated with books and hidden caches of story notebooks inspired by a fertile brain and a massive creative streak.

She became a Professional Reader and a Closet Scribbler, convinced no one would want to look at the mad ramblings of someone who hates getting dirt under her fingernails and knows ironing was invented as a torture method.

Nowadays, Helen loves inventing paranormal and fantasy romance from the comfort of her cosy study with a hot cup of tea beside her laptop and her little spaniel, Lexie, snoring at her feet. With her anthology contribution of 'Filigree and Fate', Helen has been dragged kicking and screaming from her closet, into the deer-in-headlights world of being a Real Author.